VAMPIRE FIRE

////

J.R. RAIN

12

THE VAMPIRE FOR HIRE SERIES

Moon Dance
Vampire Moon
American Vampire
Moon Child
Christmas Moon
Vampire Dawn
Vampire Games
Moon Island
Moon River
Vampire Sun
Moon Dragon
Moon Shadow
Vampire Fire

Published by
Crop Circle Books
212 Third Crater, Moon

Printed in the United States of America.

ISBN: 978-1535284400

Dedication
To H.P. Mallory and five years of friendship.

"They say hell is real. They say the devil is real, too. I say, we are all devils."
—*Diary of the Undead*

Chapter 1

"You don't have an aura," I said.

"Nor do you, Samantha Moon."

I nodded, and thought: *Touché.* I thought it because I don't usually like to say "touché," mostly because I'm not entirely sure if I'm using it correctly, or what it means, exactly. I also thought about the continuous buzzing in my head, in the space just behind my eardrum. Either a worm was burrowing into my brain, or the man sitting before me had just tripped my inner alarm system. I was betting on the latter.

His name was Buck Taggart and he was as good-looking as they came. Messy black hair. Smooth forehead that seemed devoid of lines. Powder-blue eyes. A plain white T-shirt, snug jeans, ostrich-hide boots. At least, I hoped they were ostrich. With their pale-yellow hue, they looked disturbingly similar to the rarest of the bound books I'd seen in the Occult Reading Room. Books bound in human skin.

We were at a Jamba Juice, which was my new passion these days. Drinking smoothies, that is. Tammy, the little vixen, had gotten me hooked on the blended goodness. Never had I tasted such yummy smoothness before this. Now, I was sucking down a chili mango, replete with a half-dozen boosts—because, why not?—and watching the handsome freak sitting across from me.

An hour ago, Buck had called me to request a meeting. I'd told him I had a one-hour window before I had to pick up my kids from school. I was fully intending to spend that hour at a local Jamba Juice, and told him that he was welcome to join me there, especially if he liked all things delicious.

Apparently, he liked all things delicious.

And yes, I'd chosen Jamba Juice over the last half-hour of *Judge Judy*, which should prove just... how... much... I... love... these... damned... things.

He watched me as I drank my smoothie. I watched him watching me drink my smoothie. When he'd sat across from me, he had declined my offer for a smoothie of his own, which was fine by me since I wasn't entirely sure if I had been offering to buy him one or not. To mask the awkwardness, I had suggested that it was his loss. He had only shrugged. I had noted his narrow shoulders under his T-shirt, shoulders that hinted at some muscle, but not a lot of it. I had also noted the proliferation of tattoos just inside his collar, tattoos that extended down to his elbows. Not a full sleeve, as the kids call it today. A half-sleeve. I let him watch me drink until he gave me a reason to set down my smoothie. So far, there was none. One awesome thing about being me is that brain freezes come and go in a blink of an eye.

"You are enjoying your smoothie," he said.

"More than you know."

"Would you call your need for a smoothie an obsession?"

I thought about that. "Yeah. My new obsession."

"Is a smoothie obsession common?" he asked, and, yeah, the question sounded strange to me, too.

"If not, it should be."

He nodded and a hint of a smile touched his thin lips.

I checked my cell. There was an unread text from Allison. It was going to stay unread for now. Texts from Allison tended to be needy and, well, boring. That is, unless she was off on one of her witchy adventures. Then, shit got real—and got real fast. At present, she wasn't on a witchy adventure. She was undoubtedly sitting on her couch between psychic hotline phone calls, and bored.

I said to the man sitting across from me, "I'm picking up my kids soon. I suggest you speak your piece, whatever that means."

He nodded once. The gesture opened the collar of his shirt a little more, and I saw a little more of the tattoos. And from what I could see, they were as creepy as hell: horns and fangs and blood and spikes. There were skulls and tombstones.

"I'm looking for a man," he said. So far, he hadn't given me a name, and I wasn't asking. At least, not until I was done with the smoothie.

"Now we're getting somewhere," I said, coming up for air. No, I didn't need air to survive. But I needed air to suck.

"Should I wait until you are finished so that I can have your undivided attention?"

"Do whatever the hell you want," I said.

"Whatever the hell I want. Yes, I kind of like the sound of that."

Except I didn't. And I didn't like the way his eyes kind of flashed, too. Maybe they had reflected the sun or a passing car's window, but I was certain they had flashed with an inner fire. Hard to tell in the bright of day.

I said, "But if you're going to be creepy about it, then jump on your Harley, or whatever the hell you came in here on, and take a ride."

He nodded. "My apologies, Samantha Moon. I don't mean to come across as creepy. I just feel at home with you."

I didn't exactly take that as a compliment. That this bad-boy dirtbag felt comfortable around me just might have been a sign of how far I'd descended.

"Fine," I said. "So, what kind of freak are you?"

He grinned at that. "One of the freakiest."

As he spoke, I couldn't help but note that the detailed dragon tattoo that had been above his elbow was now below his elbow. And where I had previously seen its triangular head along the outside of his arm, it was now peeking at me from just inside his arm.

As I wondered what life would be like in a padded cell, I said, "Don't leave a girl hanging. What are you? Vampire? Werewolf? A hybrid of some sort? As in, you drink blood but can't stop licking yourself?"

The man flashed what he thought was a killer smile. To me, it looked terrible. No warmth. No laugh lines. No humor. Nothing but emptiness. "No, Samantha Moon. I'm none of those."

"Fallen angel?" I suddenly asked, mostly because I didn't know what the hell else was out there. I checked my cell phone. We had five minutes remaining. Good timing, too, because I'd just come to the end of my smoothie. Hashtag sadness, as Tammy would say.

My last guess got his attention, and he cocked his head a little to one side. As he did so, the dragon's head appeared around his elbow again, having done, I was certain, a full revolution around his arm.

"You're getting warmer, Samantha Moon."

I swallowed. Hard. I'd seen some freaky stuff in my time, but I was certain I'd never come face to face with a demon before. Right here at a Jamba Juice. In the sunlight, no less. On a Thursday afternoon.

He looked at me some more. I looked at him. In my peripheral vision, I noted the dragon tattoo creeping lower and lower down his arm. I reached for my Jamba Juice cup, then remembered it was empty. All over again, I was sad that it was empty. The ringing in my ear had picked up some, too. Not obnoxiously so, but it was letting me know that *here be monsters*.

Now, the man before me smiled bigger than anyone should ever smile, like ever. The corners of his lips curled up and up, and I was reminded of the body-hopping entity in Washington State, an entity that had possessed an entire family.

"You're a demon," I said.

The thing before me shook his head and continued smiling. If anything, the smile had grown in size, now stretching from ear to ear. So. Damned. Creepy.

"No, Samantha Moon. But you are close. Oh, so close."

My minivan was parked just across the way, just a hop, skip, and a jump. Except something was telling me that there was no escaping the thing in front of me. At least, not in a minivan.

With a sickening, nauseating, and terrifying dread—and feeling more fear than I had ever felt—I suddenly knew, without a shadow of a doubt, who or what was sitting across from me. How I knew this, I wasn't sure. Maybe the burning eyes. The smiling. The confidence. The living tattoo.

"You're the devil," I said.
And his smile grew bigger still...

Chapter 2

I reached for my phone again, and, with suddenly shaking fingers, I brought up the text message app—my family used WhatsApp these days, if only to confirm when and if my daughter received and read a text.

I suddenly found it nearly impossible to control my fingers as I texted: *You need to pick up your brother.*

Two red checkmarks appeared on the screen—one to indicate I had sent the message, and one to indicate the target device had received the message. Step one completed. I waited. While I waited, I refused to look up or acknowledge the person sitting across from me. My peripheral vision—which seemed to be enhanced these days—suggested that he had quit grinning like a fool. Or like a maniacal serial killer. This was probably good. No one should smile like that, ever.

My heart beat slowly, deliberately, powerfully, rocking my body, thumping in my ears, nearly drowning out the buzzing in my head, my internal warning device. I swallowed, noting that my throat was dry for the first time in ten years. A second or two later—an eternity, really, when you're sitting across from the devil—the word "Online" appeared on my screen, indicating my daughter had logged on to WhatsApp. Step two completed. Next, the two red checkmarks turned blue, indicating that my daughter had read my message. Step three completed.

Got you, I thought. I loved this app. Of course, it was usually step four that caused me headaches. That was, her responses. This one was no exception.

No way. I'm busy!!!
No arguments, young lady.
He's like a mile away!! Maybe two miles!!
Then you'd better get started.
I'm with my friends, Mom. MY FRIENDS!!
They'll understand.
FINE!!!
Thank you, sweety.
I hate you.
Love you, too.
Oh my God!! You make me like so mad!!
I also like 'made' you. Like in my womb.
Eww! Gross. Goodbye!!!!

Grinning, I clicked off the phone and set it in front of me. For a nanosecond, I'd forgotten just who I was sitting across from. That was, until I looked up into the handsome face—and the dead, unblinking eyes. The dragon tattoo was now down around his wrist.

"Sorry about that," I said, my voice squeakier and higher-pitched than it had been in a long time. I hadn't felt this rattled in quite a while.

"Kids," he said, tilting his head toward me ever so slightly.

How he knew I was texting my daughter, I didn't know. That the devil even knew I had kids was disconcerting at best. That there was even a devil in this world was a terrible, terrible, unreal, and messed-up thought. Then again, I had seen angels and demons and highly evolved dark masters. A part of me suspected I might have even met God, too, in a Denny's a long time ago, but that could have just been wishful thinking. Hell, I was friends with immortals and alchemists and witches. I'd channeled St. Germain and sat in the presence of she who might be Mother Earth, or Gaia. Why wouldn't there be a devil, too?

Because I found the idea of hell was just too far out there, even for me. Then again, wasn't I being eternally punished, too? That is, if one would call my life a punishment. After that latest round of texting with Tammy, maybe it was.

All these thoughts and more crossed my mind as I sat there in the shade, outside of Jamba Juice with a nearby Target sitting across the far side of the expansive parking lot.

"How did you know I was texting my kid?"

"You had an appointment to pick up your kids. I assumed you were texting one of them—"

"Or I could have been texting my sister to pick them up," I said. "You lie to me again and I get up and leave and you can go back to hell."

The smile returned, creeping slowly up his face. "Yes, Sam. I lied."

"You can read my texts."

"I can read most things."

I caught the meaning of his words. "Including minds?"

"Mortals, yes. Immortals, not so much."

"Why are you smiling like that?"

Indeed, his smile had grown bigger than ever. He looked like a cross between Jack Nicholson's Joker... and Heath Ledger's Joker. Only more insane. A woman coming out of Jamba Juice paused when she saw us, then looked sharply at me, then hurried into the parking lot.

"The smile is an unfortunate side effect."

"An unfortunate side effect of what?"

"Possession, of course."

I nearly texted everyone I knew at that moment to come here, like now. Suddenly, Allison's needy texts didn't sound so needy. They sounded heavenly, reassuring. Maybe I shouldn't have stayed. Maybe I should have gotten up and left. But two things kept me here: First, I wasn't entirely convinced he was the devil. Second, he needed help... whoever he was. I would at least hear him out. Lord help me, I would hear him out.

I reached into my purse for a packet of cigarettes. Talking to the devil seemed to warrant a smoke. Fitting, somehow. I noted my hands were still shaking as I lighted up the flame.

"But why the smiling?" I asked, inhaling and expelling a long plume of smoke. "And why so big?"

"It is a natural—and human—reaction to temporary possession, Samantha."

I exhaled another cloud of smoke and noted my bouncing knee. Okay, the smiling made sense. In a way, I was possessed, too. But I was possessed permanently. As in, I was Elizabeth's permanent host.

"So, this man is only a vessel..."

"Indeed, Sam. A temporary host."

"And temporary hosts always smile like fools?"

"They tend to, yes. It is a physical reaction to possession. The body doesn't know how else to respond. And the possessor—in this case, me—can only control so much."

"So, you're saying you have no control over the smiling?"

"None at all."

"This is just too fucking weird."

"I suspect you have seen far weirder, Samantha Moon."

He had me there. Still, I didn't like that he seemed to know that I had seen far weirder. Then again, wasn't I continuously being watched by the demoness within? Wasn't Elizabeth highly aware of everything I was doing, everything I saw or heard or thought? She was, and I didn't like that either.

"So, who's the host?" I asked.

"A willing participant."

I caught the meaning. "He's a Satanist?"

"He prefers to call himself a Theistic Satanist, but it's all the same to me, really."

"They worship you," I said.

"Oh, *yesss.* With all their little, dark hearts."

I caught the lisp. A lisp that was all too familiar to me.

"But you see, Samantha, little do they know that when they worship the devil, sometimes the devil comes a-knocking."

"Sometimes you possess them, you mean."

"Sometimes I do what I want with them, *yesss.*"

"And what will you do with him?" I asked, gesturing to the possessed bad boy sitting across from me.

"We'll have some fun, Sam. He's a good-looking enough fellow. We'll meet some women. We'll get drunk and do drugs and get fucked up. I'll have more sex than even he can handle. Then, I think, we'll ride off into the sunset. Or over a cliff. I haven't decided which."

"You can possess anyone who worships you?"

"Anyone, any time."

"And you can do with them as you please?"

"*Yesss.* I like the way you say that. Say it

again."

I ignored him. "And let me guess," I said, gesturing to the sleeping serpent, "the dragon is your calling card. Yes, you might jump from body to body, but the tattoo sticks with you."

"My, aren't you a clever little girl."

"I might be little. But I'm no girl."

"No, of course. You're a full-grown vampire who has my full interest."

"Is that supposed to scare me?"

The narrow eyebrow bunched up, perhaps even comically so, as if the creature animating the human was sort of overdoing it on the facial expressions. "Why, no, Samantha Moon. It was supposed to intrigue you. Perhaps even entice you."

"Um, no."

"Worth a shot."

The afternoon shadows were shifting with the moving sun. My right leg was now exposed to the direct sunlight. Although I was wearing my day ring —forged from a much bigger medallion—sunlight still felt uncomfortable, at best, even through my jeans. I re-crossed my legs out of the sun. My movement caught his attention.

"Your rings are very useful," he said.

"Sure are."

"But not perfect."

"Good enough," I said.

"The magic that forged them is strong, but the entity within you resists them, as it will do for all time, forever more."

"What's your point?"

"I can help you defeat her."

"That's a big nope."

"Or I can give you more power than you'd ever dreamed—"

"If you can give me the power to clean skid marks out of a teenage boy's underwear, then we are in business. Otherwise, give it up, I'm not interested."

He did give it up, and seemed amused by my reactions. "You are okay with the thing living inside you?"

"For now. We have an agreement."

"Which is?"

"None of your business. So, what does the devil want with me?"

He grinned, and he kept on grinning, bigger than ever. "Like I said, I'm looking for a man, and I want you to find him."

Chapter 3

I wished like crazy I could report that this had been nothing more than a dream. Or that I might be lying in a hospital bed in a coma. Or banging around in a padded cell, my brain too far gone to know reality from make-believe.

Terrible as it was to say, one could hope.

For now, I said, "Only immortals lack an aura."

"This is the case, Samantha."

"I was led to believe the man sitting before me, the man whose body you currently possessed, was recently a human, a worshiper of you, in fact. An aura, I am told, is a soul's spillover. As in, there's more soul than the body can contain. But once immortality takes hold, a soul retreats into the body, caged forever more."

"Not quite right, Sam. Once immortality takes hold, a soul is cut off from its source."

"You mean from God," I said.

"You said it, not me."

"Is the man sitting across from me immortal now?" I asked.

"He is, in a way. But I do not choose to retain this body and I will do away with him sooner, rather than later."

He was, in essence, temporarily immortal, which sounded like a helluva oxymoron.

"Can he hear you now?" I asked.

"He can, somewhere."

"Does he know he will die soon?"

"He does."

"Does he regret allowing you inside?"

"Oh, yes. He's realizing now that it will prove to be a most catastrophic mistake."

"Is there a chance you will let him live?"

"None."

"And you are given free rein to murder humans?"

"Only the humans who invite me in."

"Because they asked for it."

"Something like that."

We were silent. I had long since dashed out my cigarette. I asked, "How does the devil lose someone?"

"It doesn't happen often. Then again, you can't lose something you never had."

"What does that mean?"

"It means the person I was expecting never arrived."

"Expecting in hell?"

"Yes, hell."

"But there is no hell," I said. I knew this, believed this, was told this over and over again during my quiet moments of automatic writing, moments when I asked questions of the Universe... and received powerful messages.

"A common misconception, Sam. Truth was, the religious leaders of yesteryear had it right. The authors of the Bible and other holy texts had it right. The Renaissance painters who painted such frightening images of hell had it right. Your movies and books have it right. Your TV shows have it right. Hell is real, Sam Moon. I am a testament to that."

"Or you're a crazy piece of shit who needs a serious ass-kicking."

"Oh, I've needed an ass-kicking for quite some time, Sam. The problem is, there's no one to do it."

I found myself feeling a bit dizzy, disoriented, but I powered through. It was important I power through, and it was also important that I hear him out, whatever or whoever he was. I couldn't go the rest of my life wondering if I really had met the devil or not. He was here for a reason, that much was obvious. He needed me for something—to locate a man—that much was obvious. But why he did, I didn't know. And who that man was, I didn't know that either. Admittedly, how said man had escaped the devil fascinated me.

And it also fascinated *her*. As in, Elizabeth, the

entity within me. But she was not clamoring to get out, oddly enough. No, she was watching from the shadows of my mind, curious, cautious.

More dizziness swept over me.

Too weird, I thought. *Too weird even for me.*

Finally, I asked: "How could a God of love punish his children in hell for all eternity? That's the problem I have with hell. That's the problem anyone has with hell."

"I said the writers and painters of yore had it right. Same with your modern visionaries as well. But I didn't say they had all the details right."

"So, hell is real, but just not how it was imagined?"

"Oh, it's exactly how it's imagined. Down to the fiery T."

I caught the slight emphasis. The tattoo dragon was watching me closely, black eyes unblinking...

"It's how they *imagined*," I said. "*Imagine* being the operative word here."

"Indeed," said the entity across from me, bowing his head slightly.

"Everyone imagines hell differently, I assume," I said.

"You assume correctly, Sam."

"Hell is not a singular place."

He nodded again. "On the surface, yes. To those who find themselves there, yes. But, in fact, it is a multifaceted, multifarious, multi-layered, multidimensional destination that's large enough, complex enough, rich enough, expansive enough to accommodate each and everyone's very own version of hell."

Okay, now my head was really spinning. In fact, I wanted another smoothie. Hell, I *needed* another.

Instead, I heard myself asking: "And how do these individual versions of hell come into existence?"

The entity sitting across from me cocked his head a little. So did the dragon on his forearm. "Through the imagination, Sam. Thoughts are things. Even hell."

"Then how do you fit in?" I asked.

"I came forth to fulfill a role."

"Because enough people believed in the devil."

"Even if the belief was subtle, Sam. Just giving voice to it, giving words to it, giving stories to it, is enough to call me into existence, as well as you and your kind. A millennium ago, there were no vampires."

"But where did you come from?" I asked.

"I'll answer your question with one of my own: Where do you think you come from, Sam?"

"I don't know," I said. "I assume from God."

He spread his hands a little.

I blinked, absorbing the implications. "You're telling me that you were born just like anyone else and, what? One day you found yourself the devil?"

"No, Sam. I am only telling you that I, too, am from God, although my role in this life, this universe, is far different than yours. From anyone's.

As such, I am not made of the same things, so to speak. Take your planet Earth. Gaia is a living, breathing thing, with a soul far more powerful than any would believe, with a role very different than your own, but yet, not so different, either. She, too, is from God, and she, too, will evolve in her own right."

"So, you're telling me you are here to fulfill a role," I said.

"Yes, Sam."

"To be the devil."

"Oh, yes."

"I assume you perform your job well."

"You have no idea."

I drummed my fingers on the metal table, which had been slowly heating up with the angling sun.

"And you need my help?"

"I do."

"Because you lost someone."

"In a word, yes."

"Who did you lose?"

The devil blinked and waited and grinned.

"It's someone I know, isn't it?" I asked.

The devil said nothing, although he leveled his full stare at me, which was terrible. Just fucking terrible.

"Someone who thought they were going to hell," I said.

"Very good, Sam."

"But never made it there."

"Correct again."

I thought about it, thought about it hard, which was damn difficult to do with this bastard sitting across from me, staring at me, when it hit me, and it hit me like a ton of bricks. I gasped. Nearly palmed my forehead.

But I didn't. Mostly I kept myself under control when I said, "You're looking for Danny."

And now, the smile began creeping up again, and it kept creeping up when the devil said, "Danny Moon has been a bad, bad boy."

Chapter 4

"But I don't understand," I said. "Danny died two years ago."

"This I know, Sam. I also know that he haunted the cavern he was killed in. But I'm not looking for his ghost. No, I am looking for *him*, his true self, his soul, his spirit. Not his discarnate memory."

"A ghost is a memory?" I asked, just to ask something, just to give myself some time to wrap my head around what I was being told.

"I am surprised you do not know this, Samantha."

"I'm, ah, still relatively new to this," I said. Danny was missing? What the hell did that mean, anyway? I swallowed, composed myself. "And no one has explained ghosts to me; at least, not really."

"A ghost is a funny thing. We mentioned that you, as a vampire, are cut off from the greater part of yourself, yes?"

"Yes."

"A ghost operates similarly. It is a memory that is cut off from the soul, as well. As a memory, it can behave like the person. It can even try to manifest and live and act as it did in life. Or it can sit around and do nothing. Eventually, it will fade into oblivion, for even a ghost will forget its true nature. And once it forgets, it ceases to exist. As you might suspect, I have no interest in ghosts."

"But you have an interest in Danny Moon?"

"Oh, yes, Sam. I have a special place in hell reserved just for him. In fact, you could call it his own private hell. You see, he was particularly creative in his ideas about hell, and I am eager to see his expectations through to the end."

I shuddered, and discovered I had broken out in a cold sweat. Yes, I sweat. Sometimes, profusely. Yes, Danny was a shit, all the way to the end, in fact, but he didn't deserve to be tortured in hell, did he?

"What end?" I asked.

"The end of his time with me, Sam. However long that may be."

"What does that mean exactly?" I asked.

"Yes, it is true that many create their own private hell, but their time with me is limited, sadly."

"Limited to how long?"

"Oh, that is based on many factors, Ms. Moon. Belief is the key here. If they *believe* they will be with me for all eternity, I give them a taste of that experience. Although they are with me for only a short period, I provide them a sense of eternity, so to speak."

"But they are not with you for an eternity..."

"It will seem like it for some. Or damn close to it. But each experience of hell is different. Each is unique, and most are very, very terrible, I must say. Our motto is to over-promise and over-deliver. Rarely do I disappoint."

"I get it. You're a creep and you like hurting people."

He shook his head, his eyes flashing. Literally. "You misunderstand, Sam. I am fulfilling a role. I have literally been summoned into existence by humans to perform this role. I have been created to be of service."

"The service of torment," I said.

"The service of expectation. I did not ask mortals to create hell. Nor did I ask them to create the devil. But they did, and here I am."

"Looking for one lost soul who skipped out on his own version of hell."

"Exactly."

"And how is it that you are aware of his version of hell?"

"Thoughts are things, Sam. Hell is real, if you believe it. Demons are real, if you believe in them. The devil is real, if you believe in him. You have a saying in your world: 'Build it and they will come.' In my world, we say, 'Believe it and they will come.' And they do come, nearly every time."

"Nearly?" I asked.

"Some slip through the cracks of space and time."

"Like Danny?"

The devil nodded once, curtly, and didn't seem capable of hiding his irritation. I wasn't sure if I should be happy or sad that Danny boy had figured out a way to elude the Prince of Darkness himself.

I asked, "And for those who believe in heaven? Worthy of love and peace?"

The devil cocked his head. "Oh, I never see them, Sam. You could say they aren't even on my radar. Religion has been both a blessing and a hindrance to my cause. Although religion has helped proliferate hell and the devil, humans also find salvation within temple walls."

I had a sudden idea, although there was a chance it had been prompted by Elizabeth. "And where do the dark masters fit into all of this?" I asked.

The devil frowned—or tried to frown—since he was currently grinning like a circus clown. "They are problematic, Sam. They have been banished to a place and time that I do not yet have access to. But I am ever hopeful, and I am patient."

"Which place and time?" I asked.

"The universe is far bigger than anyone could ever know, even the Creator."

I blinked at that.

"Oh, does that surprise you, Sam? That the one

you call God is so vast that even He, to this day, is still exploring his farthest reaches?"

I might have blinked again at this.

"Why do you think you are here? Why do you think I am here? We are here, created, to help this God to explore who he really is."

"I'm not sure I'm following..."

"All life, even mine, is from the Creator. We are living extensions, and as such, we have a job to do."

"To explore?"

"And to experience. To live and play and continue pushing the boundaries of who He is."

"And some of these boundaries lie outside of what He knows?"

"Outside and inside, Sam. For all exists within the Creator."

"And this Creator is limitless?"

"So far, yes."

"What does that mean?"

"It means He hasn't found His end."

"Are you the enemy of God?"

The devil laughed. "I am he, Sam. And so are you."

"Jesus."

"Him, too."

I drummed my longish, pointy nails along the metal table. I might have dented the surface. "And these dark masters. They are somewhere safe from you?"

"In a word, yes." He paused, and I sensed he

wanted to take my hand, but he resisted. "But let me ask you this, Sam: Is your world safe from them? Trust me, they have caused torment on par with even my own work. They have fomented hatred and rage and revenge. Trust me when I say that each and every one of them deserves their own private hell."

We were silent. The dragon tattoo seemed to be moving faster now, winding over the forearm with just enough speed that I could actually see it moving. I wanted to rub my eyes, but I didn't want to give the devil the satisfaction of knowing I was questioning my vision... or sanity.

"And God allows people to suffer in hell?"

"God gives humans the ability to create."

"Even their own versions of hell?"

"Exactly."

"And what happens after a soul leaves hell?"

"It moves on to their true destiny."

"Which is?"

"I do not know, Sam. But I do know that some will find the peace they seek, and find the loved ones they miss, and will have learned the errors of their ways. Ideally, they emerge from the hell experience better people, more evolved people, and ready to give this thing called life a go again."

"You said some?"

"Indeed, Sam. Others are truly lost souls, so evil, and so broken, as to never hope to be fixed."

"And what happens to these souls?" I asked.

"It is assumed they return straight to God, to be

absorbed... and forgotten."

Absorbed and forgotten seemed like a terrible fate. I thought about this, and suddenly wishing I had another chili mango smoothie. Perhaps it was all this talk of the fires of hell.

I said, "So, you're here to hire me to help you find my ex-husband's lost soul?"

"Yes and no, Sam. I'm not here to hire you. I'm here to bargain with you. If you give me your ex-husband, you will save a life. Perhaps you even two lives."

"Two lives? I don't understand."

"I seek Danny Moon and another."

"Who's the other?"

"You will know soon enough who, Sam."

"Fine," I said, and it occurred to me that the devil just might have gotten a glimpse into the future. Or not. Maybe he was just that good at orchestrating lives. The ultimate puppet master. "So, how does someone run from the devil?"

"There are really only two ways to run—or hide—from the devil. You already know the first, and you are intimately aware of the second, Sam."

I raised my eyebrow at that, but he was right. I knew that the highly evolved dark masters had sought refuge outside of space and time, beyond the devil's reach, in a place even he was unaware of. But Elizabeth, the entity within me, wasn't outside of space and time, was she? No, she was here, with me now, no doubt listening to all of this, including my own thoughts.

I nodded and said, "Possession."

"Very good, Sam Moon."

The idea that Danny was presently possessing someone was a disturbing one. But I had an objection. "Then why don't all souls hide from you?" I asked. "Why don't all souls possess another, if only to escape hell?"

"Because only a few know how to truly possess. Only a few know how to delve deep enough and integrate fully enough, to escape my detection."

"Such as dark masters," I said.

"Indeed," said the devil.

"Except Danny was no dark master," I said. "Trust me."

This seemed to amuse the devil, but with the hideous grin of his, it was hard to tell. "Let me ask you: How long was Danny in the company of the female vampire?"

He was talking about Detective Hanner. I considered his question. Near the end of Danny's life, he had teamed up with Hanner, my one-time friend. That they had conspired to kill me was the reason for the "one-time" part. Among other things that Hanner had done to Fang.

"I don't know," I said. "A few months, maybe?"

"Long enough to get him in trouble, I suspect," said the devil.

"Trouble how? What the devil do you mean?"

"The devil means that your Danny boy was a

dark master in training."

I was about to speak, but I couldn't. I just couldn't. I just sat there, mouth open, looking like a dope, while the devil stared at me unblinkingly, his pet dragon inching along his forearm.

Inching and inching.

***

Finally, he went on. "The highly evolved dark masters, such as the entity within you, are powerful indeed. More powerful than even you might realize. Consider this: they have fully escaped my reach, and exist outside of time and space. Additionally, they are beyond my reach even now."

"What do you mean?"

"If, say, you were to find yourself on the wrong end of a silver dagger, the entity within you would simply slip into the netherspheres, and thus, slip through my fingers yet again. But not so for Danny boy."

"Because he wasn't a full dark master," I said, and still, the thought of Danny being anything other than the sniveling, cheating, rotten husband he had been, was nearly impossible to wrap my brain around.

"You are correct, Sam. The less-evolved dark masters, as in, those who perished before their training became complete—such as the fate of your husband—can still do some damage."

"They can still possess, you mean?"

"Indeed, Sam. But the good news is, they are not beyond my reach. They are in hiding. I need only to find them."

"And what do you do when you find them?"

"Oh, it can get very messy, Sam. Very messy."

"You kill the host," I said.

"Well, I can't kill anything, Sam. Not really. But I can influence others to do very bad things to them."

"Such as murder them."

He said nothing. He didn't have to.

I drummed my fingers on the metal table, denting the crap out of it. "You said I could save two lives."

"Indeed, Sam."

"Why do you care if I save two lives? Sounds like you have this all worked out. Find the escapee, kill the host, drag the offending soul back to hell."

"I do not care, quite frankly. I wasn't created to care. But I was created to fill hell."

My investigator instincts kicked in. Throw out all this bullshit supernatural mumbo-jumbo, and in the end, this was just another missing person case. "You are offering two lives for his one."

"Two is better than one, Sam. Now, do we have a deal?"

"Who is the second person?" I asked.

The devil's eyes flashed again. "You will know soon, Sam. Even as we speak, my pet is orienting on them now."

"Your pet?" I asked.

"Perhaps *pets* is a better word," said the dark prince of hell.

And just as the words left his mouth, the dragon on his forearm reared back, and let loose with a small blast of fire.

Real fire, and real smoke.

Chapter 5

I met the devil today, I wrote in the AOL instant chat window.

It was late and I was in my living room with my laptop on my lap and a cup of coffee nearby. Earlier, when the kids had gone to bed, I had feasted on a packet of pig and cow blood. Foul stuff, surely, but at least it kept the demoness within me weak, which was how I preferred her.

If written by anyone else, I would assume they were being dramatic. Please tell me you're being dramatic, Moon Dance.

I wish I were.

The devil?

Yes.

Okay, let me process this information.

Trust me, I've been processing it all day.

Did he have horns, a pitchfork?

No, and no. But he did have a dragon tattoo.

A short pause, then: *Okay, Moon Dance. Maybe you should tell me about it.*

So, I did... from my first sip of my chili mango smoothie, to the mini-explosion of fire from the dragon tattoo...

***

I'm not sure I needed all the lurid details of your chili mango smoothie, Moon Dance, he wrote after I had finished typing my long, slightly rambling, although surprisingly mistake-free, retelling of my encounter with the devil outside Jamba Juice. *But the rest of it is... fascinating.*

Do you think he really was the devil? I wrote.

I am leaning toward that he might be the real deal, based on your description and experience.

I am, too.

How much did he know about your life?

He seemed to have a comfortable handle on what I was and what I had become.

Could he communicate with you telepathically? Or you with him?

No, and I didn't try.

I would have been surprised if you could, Moon Dance. We are closed off to other immortals, even, apparently, the devil.

Even closed off to God?

I don't know, Sam.

I wrote: *The angel, Ishmael, can still*

communicate with me telepathically.

He was once connected to you, Sam. I suspect he was granted special access. After all, what use is a guardian angel if that angel can't intimately and accurately know the very stupid decision someone is about to make?

And the alchemist, I wrote. *He can hear my thoughts.*

The alchemist is using powerful magicks that neither you nor I understand.

And what about Tammy? She can hear anyone and everyone. No one is safe from my daughter.

Your daughter might be an in-betweener, Sam. Same with your son. They are expanding into something truly unheard of—and unseen—as far as my own research goes.

I knew Fang's own research was as extensive as it came, perhaps second only to the Alchemist's own knowledge. Fang, I knew, was dying to enter the Occult Reading Room. Thus far, he'd not been granted access, for reasons unknown to me.

I wrote: *I'm leaning toward God having access to my thoughts. I mean, he's the Creator of all, am I right? What could be hidden from him? Or her? Or whatever he or she is.*

But the devil doesn't? asked Fang.

The devil didn't seem very different from you and I. And he definitely didn't seem very different from the demon that possessed the Thurman family on Skull Island. His influence and range seemed to be contained somewhat.

Unless someone invites him in, wrote Fang.

Exactly, I wrote. *Then all bets are off, and your life is in his hands.*

And they've been looking for Danny all this time?

I assume yes.

Any chance Danny went to, you know, heaven? Maybe he found salvation just before death? Maybe he repented and begged for mercy?

He was helping to lure me to my death, if that says anything.

But what if he thought killing you was truly the right thing to do? To destroy what some think of as evil?

I shrugged in my own living room, although Fang couldn't see me do so.

The devil didn't think so, I wrote. *The devil seemed to think a very special hell had been waiting—and still is waiting—for Danny, fashioned after my ex-husband's own particular beliefs. Apparently, Danny was very afraid of hell, and suspected he was going straight to it. Apparently, Danny had done something far worse than I—or anyone—knew. Apparently, and this is according to the devil, Danny was a big deal in the sex-and-drug trade in San Bernardino County. He both loved what he did, and hated himself for being a part of it, and, according to the devil, Danny had hurt a number of people, killing some, too.*

Jesus. Your ex sounds like a real peach. Well, please tell me that you laughed in the face of the devil, and told him to go back to hell?

I said nothing. Or wrote nothing. The cursor in my IM window blinked, waiting.

Moon Dance? came Fang's words a minute later. *Moon Dance, please tell me that you didn't make a deal with the devil. Especially a deal for that shithead ex-hubby of yours.*

Still, I didn't respond.

Moon Dance?

Chapter 6

I was alone in my office.

My kids were asleep and it was hours before dawn and I was staring down at a mostly blank piece of paper. That there was a real devil out there, I now had no doubt. There were angels, and demons, and ghosts, and witches, and vampires, and werewolves, and magical tattoos, and God knows what else. Was it really a stretch to believe that there might be a devil, too?

"Yes," I said aloud. "Yes, it is."

Mostly because it went against everything I believed about the universe. I did not believe that a god of creation would punish his creations for choosing poorly, as I had been taught in Sunday School. Choose Christ, and go to Heaven. Choose anything else, and suffer in hell. I had rejected the notion at an early age, as it felt false to me.

But the devil's explanation made a kind of sense, too. And my own reason for existence had been explained to me similarly. With enough thought and belief behind anything, that thought or belief is summoned into existence. Well, there was certainly a lot of thought and belief in and around the devil. And hell, too, for that matter. And not just thought and belief, but a real fear, all of which gave the devil more power.

That each hell was personal, and modified to fit the expectation and belief of the soul, was beyond my comprehension. If so, there were literally billions of hells out there.

All managed by the devil and his minions.

Too weird, I thought. *Just too damn weird.*

No, I had not made a deal with the devil, but I had told him I would think about it, and that's what I was doing now. Thinking hard. On top of my paper were the words *Pros* and *Cons*, with a line drawn down the middle. So far, there was nothing else on the page.

The devil's offer had been basic: two lives for one. Who the *two* lives were, I didn't know. But the *one* was Danny's soul. I could live with that part of the deal.

I had asked what the catch was, and the devil had laughed, throwing back his head, as the dragon on his arm snorted out another lick of flame. When he was done laughing, he mentioned something about being unfairly blamed for one-sided deals, deals that always favored him, in the end. I asked if there was any truth in that, and he had said maybe, and laughed again, which didn't exactly ease my apprehension.

I told him I also took checks, and gold bars, and he had laughed at that, too. The devil, apparently, only bartered. And had a sense of humor, to boot. Go figure.

I had told the devil I would think about it. He had nodded, smiled far bigger than was necessary, and sauntered off to, you guessed it, a Harley-Davidson parked not too far away.

And, like the original rebel that he was, the devil roared off without a helmet... and with reckless abandon.

***

The pros and cons were fairly obvious.

Pro: I saved two lives.

Con: my bastard ex-husband would serve an apparently well-deserved and expected sojourn in his own private hell. Perhaps that was a pro in some people's book, but I did believe in forgiveness, even if the demon bitch inside of me craved revenge. And she did, too. I felt it. I felt her objection deep within my mind.

Pro: Danny wouldn't actually suffer in hell for all eternity, which was actually a pro in my book. Hell, I did have two kids with the guy. But he would suffer just long enough to satisfy his own version of hell.

Con: How could I trust the devil? How could I trust any of this? I needed, of course, a second opinion.

I considered all whom I might call upon, and only one name rose to the surface.

Tomorrow, I thought, when I looked at the time. Dawn was just a half hour away, and already I was feeling the weight of sleep creeping over me. *Tomorrow, I will summon my guardian angel.*

My *ex*-guardian angel.

Ishmael.

Chapter 7

"You did say three-headed?" I asked.

"I did, Sam. I did, and I really wish I hadn't."

It was just before noon—and I wasn't happy about that. Usually, I'm sleeping now. Usually, it takes two alarm clocks and a little luck to get me up around 1:30 p.m. But on this morning, my cell had rung incessantly. I didn't always hear my cell ringing, but the caller had been persistent. The caller knew they had to be persistent to raise me from the dead. The caller had been, of course, Detective Sherbet.

"Where was it spotted?" I asked. I was holding my travel container of coffee, which I sipped from now. I was pretty sure the coffee did nothing for me. But I believed it did, and that belief was good enough.

"Heading south on Lemon Street, between

Rosecrans and Chapman, before it disappeared."

I nodded. Then nodded again, digesting this. "And when you say disappeared, you mean it literally... disappeared," I said.

Detective Sherbet looked pained. And maybe a little sick. His usually ruddy jowls were white, accentuated by splotches of red. The haunted look in his bloodshot eyes suggested that he might have chosen the wrong career path. At least on this day.

"That's what the reports say, Sam. A three-headed dog, running down the middle of the road, in the suicide lane, to be exact. It paused once and let out a terrifying roar. One woman had a heart attack, right there at the bus station. There were no less than six serious car accidents. After pausing, the creature continued south, picking up speed, its center head looking forward while its two..." Sherbet loosened his collar. "While its two other heads looked off to either side. Their eyes were, according to most reports..."

"Were what?"

"I don't want to say it, Sam. Don't make me say it."

"Say it," I said.

He looked down at thick hands that were now clasped over his rotund belly. He nodded, and then seemed to accept all over again that his life would never, ever be the same again. At least, not since meeting me.

"Their eyes were on fire. Burning eyes on a three-headed dog that disappeared into thin air. But there's more."

I waited. We were in his downtown office at the Fullerton Police Department, just a hop, skip and jump from Lemon Street, the scene of the three-headed sighting. The old police station still retained some of its Spanish architectural charm, with swooping archways and lots of plaster. Inside was another story. Hi-tech, fast-paced, glass offices filled the expansive space. Fullerton sported 150,000 residents, and not all of them were law-abiding citizens. At last count, Fullerton averaged about a homicide a month. Enough to keep Sherbet and his team busy.

"Busier since I got to know you, Sam."

I chuckled. He didn't. Yes, Sherbet was one of the few mortals who had immediate access to my thoughts. I was about to say "complete access," but that wasn't correct. No, he only had access to my current thoughts; that is, what I was thinking now. What I was feeling now. Or, in this case, what I was noticing now, even if in random passing. My deeper, richer, scarier, secretive thoughts were not available. Indeed, such thoughts would only be available to maybe the alchemist, my ex-guardian angel, my daughter, and the bitch within me, from whom I held no secrets.

"You said there was more, Detective," I prompted. Yes, I could have dipped into his thoughts and found the information, but I didn't dip when I didn't have to. And I rarely dipped with personal friends. It seemed rude, intrusive, and overly impatient. Plus, I wanted my friends to have their own secrets.

"Some described it as having a pointed tail, a few called it a dragon's tail, in fact. Almost all claim it was as big as the biggest horse."

"Maybe it was a horse," I said. "Maybe someone was pulling a stunt. How hard would it be to find two fake horse heads and have them hanging off either side? And, for that matter, hook up red lights—"

Sherbet was shaking his head. "Sam, you have no idea how much I want to believe your theory. I was thinking something similar. The problem is, each and every witness, to a person, claim it was a really big dog—a cross between a Rottweiler and some sort of... hellhound."

His last word caught me by surprise, so much so that I made sure to quickly shield my thoughts.

"You okay, Sam?" asked Sherbet, suddenly looking concerned... and maybe a little suspicious. "Your usual inane flow of thoughts was just cut off..."

"It's nothing, Detective. At least, not anything I am willing to discuss now. And, ouch, about the inane part. How many witnesses?"

"Twenty-eight, so far. With more coming in."

"Video?"

"None, although a few people tried. Nothing shows up on film. Sam, please tell me it's one of your own."

"One of my own?"

"You know, one of your friends or something."

"I don't have any three-headed dog friends, Detective."

"Can any of them, you know, turn into one? Yes, I just heard myself. And I hate that we are having this conversation."

"The answer, Detective, is that, no, I don't know what your witnesses saw. And, no, none of my friends can turn into a three-headed dog."

With my thoughts still shielded from Sherbet, I recalled the devil's words from yesterday: *Perhaps pets is a better word...*

Wasn't the three-headed dog, Cerberus, the official mascot of hell? It was, and if my scant knowledge of Greek mythology was correct, the city of Fullerton might have been introduced to the devil's pet... or pets.

"Will it come back, Sam?"

"I don't know."

"Do you know why it's here?"

I waited before saying, "I might."

"Jesus, Sam."

We were quiet some more. The air conditioner kicked in. Cool air on my cold skin was redundant. The detective looked like he might pass out.

"Are you okay, Detective?" I asked.

"No, Sam."

"Are you just being dramatic?"

"This three-headed fucking horse thing is going to be the death of me."

"Okay, now you're being dramatic."

He ignored me. "The people in the station... they're saying it's some sort mythical creature. Cerebral or something."

"Cerberus," I corrected.

"Sam, this isn't happening."

"Do you want me to hold you?" I asked.

"Do not hold me, Sam."

I shrugged. "Your loss."

"I need your help, Sam."

"I think you do."

Chapter 8

An hour later, I met Sandy Damayanti in a Rite Aid parking lot on Lemon Street.

She was a witness who had curiously asked to see me by name. Her name and contact info had been provided by Sherbet, who seemed befuddled by her request.

Anyway, for someone who had seen a three-headed devil dog, she didn't come across as particularly shaken up. If anything, she seemed excited by the prospect of hell on earth. She wore black yoga pants and black New Balance shoes. Her tank top was pink. She wore a tight sports bra under her tank top. She was cute and friendly and maybe a little ditzy, which I wasn't in the mood for. At least not in the middle of the day, when I am at my crankiest.

We stood in the shade of a jacaranda tree with

its purple flowers and the buzzing bees. One thing people forget about vampires: we can still hurt, even if it's only temporary. I was careful around the bees. I had asked Sandy to tell me what she saw, which she did now.

"I was in the Rite Aid, picking up my prescription—do you need to know my prescription?"

"No."

"Well, it was b.c., just in case you do. You never know, right?"

"Right."

"Anyway, I was coming out to my car when I heard all the screaming and the cars braking and then the cars smashing into each other. Do you need to know the shoes I was wearing?"

"I do not."

"I was wearing my Skechers with the pink heart design—oh, my God, so cute."

I looked at her. "How is this relevant?"

"Because I was wearing them last night, silly. I mean, officer."

"I'm not an officer. I'm a consultant to the Fullerton Police Department."

"Oh, right. Gotcha."

I doubted she got it. Or anything, for that matter. Okay, that might have been rude.

My consulting gig with the Fullerton Police Department was an unusual one for a private investigator to have. Years ago, I'd been brought in to help find a particularly sadistic serial killer.

Turned out the bastard was running a blood bank, whose donors were not willing participants. I still had flashbacks of the victims hanging from meat hooks, flashbacks that I think the bitch within me rather enjoyed... and perhaps even triggered. Anyway, in the world of vampires, blood donors didn't need to be killed. In fact, it was better that our victims didn't die, better that they forget and move on, as proven by Fang and his own successful bloodletting operation he called a bar. Blood banks such as his did good work. It kept many of our local bloodsuckers from feeding on people and their kids. It also put a little cash in Fang's pocket. Or a lot of it. It also plugged him into the local vampire scene, which sometimes proved invaluable to me and my investigations.

So, my job title as police consultant stuck, and I was even on the Fullerton Police Department's payroll, from which I collected a few dollars each month. Which meant I was at their beck and call. Which also meant that Sherbet could yell at me even more than usual.

"Who's Sherbet?" asked Sandy Damayanti.

Oops.

"No one," I said. "Just thinking out loud. Now, walk me through what you saw."

"Sure!" she said a little too excitedly. "I was just coming out of Rite Aid, after picking up my b.c.—"

"What's b.c.?" Then it hit me. *Birth control.* Geez.

I nearly told her to continue on, but decided there was a better way. So, at the risk of awakening the bitch within me, I gave Sandy Damayanti a silent command to be quiet and open her mind to me. Why have her retell the story, when I could relive it? In her memories, that is.

Her mouth shut and her eyes flickered a little, and I should have felt like shit taking over her mind, but I didn't. Neither did the bitch within, who had perked up a little.

Slipping past her surface forethoughts proved to be challenging. In fact, I encountered quite a bit of opposition... so much so that I nearly gave up. There was something... pushing against me, resisting me, denying me. Or trying to. But there, between the folds of her thoughts, I finally found an opening.

At the second layer of thought, where memories are usually stored, I found something else entirely. It was, I was certain, another presence. It was hovering there, just beyond her conscious mind, watching, alert, a floating black blob on the sea of her simple thoughts. It sensed me and scurried deeper into her mind, and I let it go. I wasn't here to exorcise any demons, or whatever the hell that had been.

Here, in this place of memories, I asked her to recall back to last night, and she did. The dull, formless, random memories dispersed, making room for the shiny new memories from just the night before.

Next, I told her to start from the beginning, minus the damn shoes and birth control prescription. She did, although I sensed a reluctance within her to not talk about her cute Skechers. But my own will now usurped her own, to the unending delight of the demoness within me. The crazy, crazy bitch.

Sandy and I might have looked like two gals standing in the shade together, on a lunch break perhaps, enjoying yet another perfect Southern California afternoon. But to the keen observer, they would have noted Sandy's eyelids fluttering, her eyeballs rolling randomly in their sockets. They would have noted my own eyes being partially shut. They might have noticed my lips moving subtly as I gave Sandy sub-vocal commands. Mostly, my lips didn't move. Mostly, my commands were given on a telepathic level, but Allison had pointed out to me once that my lips tended to move, too. Go figure.

What they wouldn't have known was that I was re-living Sandy's memory from the night before, reliving them in exquisite detail, in fact.

***

She's walking up to her sporty Hyundai that looks, yes, cute.

She is having a good day, feeling good, but now, she doesn't feel so good. Now, she feels... uneasy. She looks down at her arms, and there are goosebumps there. She rubs her arms and shivers, but it's not cold. Today has been sunny and warm...

She looks into the sky...

Gray clouds. And not just gray... but swirling and gray. And, sweet Jesus... lightning! She hasn't seen lightning in, like, forever. Now, the hair on her head is standing on end, and she can feel a crazy energy crackling from seemingly everywhere. She pauses right there in the middle of the parking lot. She pauses and turns in a small circle.

Something is happening. Something crazy and wild, and she doesn't know if she should be afraid or awe-inspired. She decides both are in order.

Now, she feels it in her teeth. A ringing, zinging, high-pitched, tuning-fork sensation that she definitely knows she doesn't like. Not at all. Nope.

And that's when it happens.

Another lightning strike.

But this time, the bolt hits nearby, maybe a hundred yards away. Brakes squeal, a handful of people scream. She's one of them. Had someone not been looking into the sky, they might have missed the thunderbolt... and thought maybe a transformer had blown. But she had seen the bolt, and it struck there, just down the road.

Although afraid, she had always liked the strange, the weird, the different. After all, hadn't she often played with a Ouija board while growing up? Didn't she actually see something rise up once out of the Ouija board? Didn't she sometimes suspect those dark thoughts of hers weren't, well, hers? That they were *his*, whoever he was? In fact, it was safe to say she had never truly been the same since. Her personal relationships all failed. Her relationship with her parents deteriorated. And wasn't the root of all the problems... him? They were. She was sure of it. She had become angry and belligerent, and sometimes uncontrollable rage filled her. She tried to stamp it out. Tried to put on a brave face. But mostly, she was angry. Mostly, she was afraid. And she didn't have a damned clue what to do about it. Or about the thing within her, whatever it was.

These were her deeper thoughts, triggered by the strange events in the sky above her, now bubbling up to the surface and scaring her all over again. Because, after all, she didn't want to believe something had possessed her. But she suspected it had. And she suspected it was still there.

And now, the memory slipped away, because there was more screaming going on in the street. A lot more, and soon, she saw why.

**

As with all memories that I access, this one comes to me in real-time, as if it's happening now...

Movement appears from her left, where the lightning has struck. The movement is a *big* movement. A large shadow or something. A *glowing* shadow, which makes no sense to her mind. But there it is. Moving, rushing toward her, galloping like a horse. No, not quite a horse. The stride is off. It runs more flat-out, like a dog. A very big dog.

The shadow continues to materialize, crystallize, clarify, calcify...

The head is quite big. Too big for a normal dog's head, at least. Sandy feels like she's watching a Michael Bay movie. She has a sudden, shifting, out-of-body experience that makes her think she might actually be in a movie theater, and that maybe, just maybe she had fallen asleep in her seat and is only now awakening...

No, she thinks, actually shaking her head. This is no movie, and this is no movie theater. Dizziness grips her. But also excitement. More excitement than I, myself, was prepared for...

The charging shadow is heading toward her on Raymond Avenue, running along the center of the street, down what she thinks of as the suicide lane. It's a busy street, surrounded on both sides by shopping centers, freestanding stores, and hole-in-the-wall restaurants. Cars are stopping, swerving, crashing, honking, racing, skidding.

The creature continues to materialize. Sandy doesn't know if it, in fact, has always been out of focus and is only now coming into focus, or if her shocked mind is having a difficult time perceiving it.

She doesn't know, and she doesn't really care. At least, not now. After all, things are happening fast.

Mostly, she feels utterly and completely

excited.

The ground shudders with each thunderous footfall. She can actually feel each vibration rising up through the asphalt of the parking lot. I wonder if she is aware of her teeth rattling, too. Probably not, but I am, for I am both watching it through her perspective... and watching her watch it as well.

Strange stuff, but I have the added benefit of standing back a little and watching the events proceed... and also watching her reaction, and the reaction of the others around her, those she isn't quite aware of, but whom her senses had picked up.

For instance, I can see a man standing nearby, his back to her, a man in a white T-shirt and blue jeans and boots. A man with tattoos and, admittedly a cute butt. The winding tattoo along his left arm is familiar. I am certain it is a dragon tattoo. And I am certain, even from here, that I can see it slowly moving. Now, the man turns and looks at Sandy, and I see the huge grin on his face.

"You will meet her soon," the devil had said.

But Sandy's focus is entirely on the creature running down the middle of Raymond Avenue, not the man standing near the curb, and certainly not on his moving tattoo.

And so, I allow myself to see what she sees, and what she sees has now come into startling clarity. It is clearly a dog. The blurry, massive heads have coalesced into *three* massive heads. I was expecting it, yes, but seeing it live (and through her eyes), was disturbing nonetheless. The three pairs of eyes are, in fact, lapping flames, snapping and burning and leaving behind wispy tendrils of black smoke.

Jesus.

More cars crash. I watch a truck plow into the rear-end of a Prius. Airbags explode inside the smaller car. Sandy caught the accident, too, and I also catch her thoughts: "One less Prius..."

Okay, *ouch.*

A guy on an old ten-speed tries to stop, but the front wheel wobbles uncontrollably, and he tumbles sideways. He crab-crawls backward as the galloping dog passes him by. The dog's right head watches him, its eyes crackling and spitting fire.

Sweet, sweet Jesus...

There is a car sitting in the suicide lane, waiting to make a left turn into one of the busier shopping centers. It's also sitting directly in the path of the charging dog. The creature, I see, is about the size of the car, maybe bigger. Yes, definitely bigger. There is an elderly woman inside and she makes the sign of the cross. As the dog approaches, she covers her eyes with her hands. Sandy is fascinated to see what's going to happen next, and inches closer to the street. The rapidly approaching dog is nearly across from her. But, to her disappointment, the dog leaps over the car in a single bound, its pitch-black haunches flexing and bulging with shimmering muscle.

Shortly after that, the dog stops running. Perhaps it's only coincidence that it has stopped running opposite Sandy.

Either way, it stops... and all three heads orient on her.

***

Sandy squeaks and takes a few steps back.

The three heads are as big as dinosaur skulls, their teeth nearly as long. Their three sets of burning eyes would be enough to make anyone die of fright. How Sandy doesn't descend into panic, I don't know. Amazingly, suddenly, a big rig roars by, perhaps oblivious to the spectacle standing in the center lane. And as it passes, the dog disappears, too.

Amazingly, I sense Sandy's disappointment. Yes, she's breathing hard, but she's also excited. She feels validated somehow. She feels alive. She feels like anything is possible. All by seeing the world's creepiest dog. But I know what she means.

In an instant, the heavens—and hells—had cracked open for her, giving her a glimpse into the supernatural. And she soaked it in.

It is now, as she stands there by the curb, as the cars around her seem to awaken from their fugue, that she sees the man twenty feet away. The man who is watching her... and grinning. She misses the tattoo on his forearm, the tattoo curling slowly around and around...

I considered exiting her mind.

But first, I had a job to do...

***

To the world, we were just two women chillaxing under the shade of the jacaranda. Little did the world know that one woman, me, was deep inside the other woman's mind.

Deep, deep inside.

After all, I was presently chasing down the darkness that I had seen earlier, a darkness that had been hiding inside her all these years, a darkness that was presently running for its life...

***

It was a strange chase, indeed.

I was reminded of my own journey deep inside Russell Baker's mind, my sweet boxer boyfriend who had inadvertently become a sort of love slave of mine, thanks to the bitch inside me. The problem was, I didn't want a love slave—and to release him from the spell, I had to plunge deep into his subconscious mind, to find his true self hidden deep below the cursed layers. I managed to release him then, and have yet to speak to him since, which I had demanded and commanded. He needed to be free from me, forever—and, yeah, that kinda broke my heart.

This was similar, except there were no layers of spells to break through. It was just the wide-open expanse of her mind. A mind the entity knew well.

After all, it had been a part of her for nearly a decade. Maybe longer.

And so, it led me on a roller coaster ride through crackling synapses, swirling memories, forgotten memories, hidden fears, and unknown memories of seemingly another time and place. Past life memories, I realized. All of these I flew through, racing toward the shapeless blackness that always, always seemed just one step ahead of me.

I caught it looking back at me, its red eyes glowing and full of hate—or so I assumed—as it hung a hard right and plunged ever deeper. We were in a void now, with only an occasional flashing of yellow light, the occasional random chirp. I could have been in outer space. Where we were, exactly, I didn't know.

Her mind, I thought. *We were still in her mind.*

Another flash of light, and something appeared next to me. It was an image of Sandy herself, but she looked different in the image. She looked stronger, younger, hungrier. Now I saw the fangs hanging over her lower lip. A vampire? Granted, I didn't have such fangs myself, but the image was clearly of herself as a creature of the night.

The image grew in size, and then rushed forward and out of sight.

Another flash, and this time I saw her striding through a big, beautiful, Gothic home, with a winding staircase and tapestries and thick mohair rugs.

That image grew as well, and rushed away.

And still, I chased the shadow through this void, a void that was punctuated with the occasional burst of light... and visual appearances of something that, I suspected, had not yet happened. There she was, standing astride a pile of money. And there she was with a man hanging onto her, clearly worshiping her.

And suddenly, just like that, the shadow stopped running and turned and faced me, eyes glowing red, but not with an internal fire.

"Sssister, why do you chase me so?" it asked.

I stopped as well, and found myself floating before it in the seemingly eternal darkness.

"Who are you?" I asked. My telepathic voice seemed to have no range.

"I do not remember, sssister," it said, and we now drifted in a concentric circle, rotating together, facing each other in the darkness. "Not darkness, Sssamantha Moon. Thisss is where dreams are born. It is a beautiful place, is it not? I visit here often."

The entity was humanoid, although barely so. I suspected the creature had long since forgotten its own shape, if it ever had one.

"I was human once, a long time ago..."

"Why are you here?" I asked. Nearby, another flash of light appeared, and within the light was an image of Sandy driving in a black sports car.

"I am here to live again, Sssam. Isn't that what we all want?"

"How do you know my name?"

It did not immediately answer me, and we

drifted and turned in this netherspace of creation—all while my physical body huddled in the shade and Sandy's upturned eyes shuddered inside her skull.

"In here, there are no secrets, Sssam. In here, we are one mind."

I considered its words. My own thoughts were certainly safe from most immortals. Not so safe from humans, some of whom I inadvertently opened up to. Some of whom had gotten so close that we were intimately connected. I always assumed it was the case because such effortless telepathy was beneficial for the dark masters. In fact, most everything I could do was to benefit the dark entity within me. These were *her* powers spilling over into my life. Controlling mortals were of benefit to her. Knowing their secrets as well. But other dark masters did not see a benefit of letting those of their own kind into their minds, and, as such, shielded their thoughts from other immortals. Which is why I generally had no access to other immortals' thoughts.

But here, my mind was projected, encumbered by my immortal body, free to roam Sandy's mind, and, as such, an open book.

"Yesss..." it hissed. "Yesss... you have worked it out marvelously."

"What are you?" I asked.

"I am but a humble lost soul, looking for refuge."

"Why do you not go to the light?" I asked.

"The light does not want me, Sssam. At least not yet."

I nodded, understanding. "You are destined for hell."

"My own private hell, Sssam."

"And you are afraid," I said.

"Yesss..."

I spread my arms wide, although it was only a projection of myself spreading my arms. "And you are safe here?" I asked.

"For now, but I feel him closing in."

"Him?"

"You know the one of which I speak, for you have just met him."

"The devil?"

With that, the entity quit moving and I felt his fear, coming at me in wave after wave. I had a sudden impression. After all, he was open to me as well. It was of a ceremony, a ritual. I saw the flash of a knife blade, followed by pain... and the slipping away of life itself.

"You were in training to become a dark master," I said.

"Yesss."

"You were killed."

"For a simple mistake, Sssam. The masters do not allow for mistakes."

"This was a long time ago," I said, no doubt back around the time when Elizabeth and her fellow freaks walked the earth.

"No, Sssam. Not so long ago."

Now, I caught within him the scene of modern buildings, of the Hollywood sign. Of secret ceremonies in the Hollywood Hills. I stood back, confused. I had been under the assumption the dark masters had been banned long ago.

"The first wave, Sssam. But there is a second... and it's forming now. And it's about to break."

"How did you escape hell?" I asked, shaking my head. "How did you escape the devil?"

As I asked the question, I already sensed the answer within him. It was the dark masters who had figured out how to out-trick the devil. And the entity before me knew just enough to slip between the devil's fingers, but not enough to stay hidden forever.

"He's coming for you," I said, remembering the way the devil had looked at Sandy last night, as she had watched the three-headed dog speed by.

"It is so, Sssam."

"You don't have long now."

"Not long at all..."

I considered my options. I considered removing the entity, although I wasn't entirely sure how. Still, I suspected with enough intent, I could. Yes, the devil was closing in on him, that much was obvious. Perhaps that's why the dog had appeared. The dog had sniffed him out.

The entity before me shifted and reformed, like a living inkblot. "Please, sssister. Won't you allow me to stay a little longer? A temporary reprieve before the endless suffering?"

I considered its request, and wondered how, exactly, I had come to a place in my life where I could grant a temporary reprieve to hell itself. I could only conclude that this was all insanity. With that said, I was just about to grant its request, just about to leave it be, and allow the woman named Sandy to remain possessed by a lower dark master. A not-so-evolved dark master, when I decided that I hadn't come all this way—that is, all this way inside her mind—to come away empty-handed.

No one deserved possession, especially by what I suspected was a sniveling, slimy, destructive creature, a creature that had influenced Sandy's life for ill for the past decade, a creature that, I also suspected, had taken much from her, used her, and wanted to use her still.

I couldn't allow that, and I couldn't allow harm to come to Sandy, either. After all, the devil had made it clear that he wanted the entity within her, one way or another.

I had just reached my conclusion when the creature turned tail, but I was already moving, my hand lashing out...

And caught hold of it...

***

In the real world, I saw my physical hand opening and closing tightly.

Back in the darkest recesses of her creative imagination, the thing before me jerked and fought me, but it had no real strength. No ability to fend for itself. All it could do was run, and it was done running.

"Sssister... please... you know not what you are doing..."

I ignored its pleading and retreated back through her consciousness, back through the many layers of her mind and memories and emotions. Faster and faster I went, until I found myself blinking in my physical body, and feeling disoriented.

What I didn't expect to see was a living shadow in my hand. I was reminded of a swarm of snakes or bugs; it swirled and darted over my knuckles, but I held tight—and not quite sure what to do. I doubted others could see it. I also doubted that this was really happening.

After all, in the bright of day, in the shade of a flowering jacaranda tree, I was holding the lost and desperate soul of a dark master in training. I didn't know what to do, but I knew I wanted this oily, slimy thing as far away from me as possible.

And so, using all my strength, which may or may not have been necessary, as the thing in my hand weighed next to nothing, I heaved it high into the sky.

And as I did, I saw something I wouldn't soon forget: something winged and black and shaped vaguely like a dragon appeared in the sky. But it wasn't a dragon. It was longer, blacker, sharper.

It was a demon. An honest-to-God demon.

It snatched the undulating black form out of the air with a clawed hand... and disappeared again.

I was still looking up into the sky, seriously doubting what I had just seen, when a blue Volkswagen Beetle stopped in the road in front of me, to the chagrin and anger of those behind. The passenger-side window rolled down, and the driver, a young woman in her twenties—leaned across the seat and looked at me.

"That's one down, Sssamantha Moon," she said, and as she spoke, the smile on her face grew... and grew and grew.

Chapter 9

We were in my minivan.

I had basically exorcised an entity from the girl, and released a decade's worth of darkness from her. I had, in essence, freed her... and in the process, had sent a soul to hell. Even if only temporarily, although I didn't really know that, did I? I was, after all, taking the devil's word for how hell operated. Anyway, I had basically given the woman next to me her life back. I had freed her of a parasitic entity, and you would think she would be happy about it, relieved in fact, but you would be wrong. So very wrong.

"I feel different," she was saying again. "I feel weaker."

Minutes earlier, I had guided her to my minivan. I had needed her support as much as she needed mine. Chasing the entity through the many layers of her mind had been exhausting on a mental and psychic level. Not to mention, hauling the kicking and fighting creature out.

I said, "Weaker, how?"

She had been opening and closing her fingers. "I was always oddly strong for a girl. Hell, for anyone. I mean, not crazy strong, but usually stronger than my boyfriends. Heck, I was always the one opening the jar of pickles!"

I knew the feeling, at least with Danny. Early on, he had become very resentful that I'd grown far stronger than him. Far, far stronger.

"Then again," she added, "I usually feel a little out-of-sorts during the day."

"Out-of-sorts, how?"

"Weaker, brain foggier. I tend to sleep. My doctors didn't know what to make of it. One of them called it an early onset of sundowners syndrome. But my situation seemed to be the opposite."

I waited, and had already seen where this was going.

"At sundown, I actually felt stronger. At night, too. I always felt I was—I don't know; this is going to sound weird."

"Try me."

"Well, I always felt that I was sort of allergic to the sun itself."

"Not as weird as you think." A question suddenly occurred to me. "Sandy, how old are you?"

By my estimates, she looked maybe twenty-two, maybe even younger.

She blushed a little, ducked her head. "Thirty-eight. I know, I look young. Maybe it's because I avoid the sun these days. My friends call me a vampire, ha-ha."

She laughed it off, or tried to, but I saw the doubt in her eyes, the confusion. I also saw a shell of the girl I had met only a half hour earlier.

"Well, to be a true vampire," I said, doing a decent job of acting, "doesn't one, you know, drink blood or something?"

Her eyes flashed. She opened her mouth, then closed it again. I gave her a subtle suggestion to open up to me. She nodded, although I didn't think she knew she nodded.

"That's just the thing, Sam. I eat all my steaks rare. I eat one or two of them a week."

"Rare?"

"The rarer the better. Once..." She paused, looked away, and I prompted her again. "Once, I bit one of my boyfriend's lips and kept kissing him even while he..."

"While he what?"

"While he struggled and bled. I pinned him down. I was stronger than him, just by a little. He eventually threw me off him, but not before..." A pause, and another prompt by me. "But not before I drank like a lot of his blood. He was mad at me for weeks. He almost left me, but my boyfriends never do. Not until I kick them out or get restraining orders. Or my new boyfriend beats them up. It's usually messy. Funny how guys get so attached, huh?"

"Yeah," I said. "Funny."

Especially when they are love slaves, I thought.

Yeah, the girl before me had been, I was certain, a very minor form of vampire. Her powers, I was certain, were directly proportional to the entity within her. He had, after all, only been a dark master in training. The entity within me, of course, had been their strongest, or one of their strongest.

Lucky me, I thought.

The low-level dark master—or dark novice, perhaps—gave her, in effect, the best of both worlds. Unusual strength, but still a tolerance to the sun, a connection to mortal life. With only a mild need for blood, and the kind of skin most women would kill for.

"And what would happen when you ate food?" I said. "Besides rare steaks?"

"Oh, I have terrible IBS. I mean, it's kind of gross to admit it, but I can't keep a lot of food down. Sometimes I just skip eating altogether."

"But you can eat some foods?"

"Yeah, some. Most meats. Dairy foods. But almost nothing else."

"Fruits and vegetables?"

She shook her head vigorously. "They give me terrible cramps."

Again, I knew the feeling. That is, back before I had the opal ring. I took her hand and turned in my seat and faced her.

"Your hand is cold, Samantha. People used to tell me I had cold hands—"

"I know they did, Sandy," I said. "And they also told you about their dreams, and you probably had to admit that you never remember your own dreams."

She looked at me and her eyes squinted a little, then she nodded. "Yeah, I don't dream much, if at all."

"But you used to."

"All the time."

"And when you look into mirrors..." I began.

Her head snapped around and she gasped. "I never talk about that! Never told a living soul..."

"I bet you didn't."

Now, she was shaking her head, and I saw the tears appearing in her eyes. She kept shaking her head and I gave her a few seconds to work through her emotions before I prompted her to tell me about the mirrors.

She did, and I could relate, although her own unique experience would have been far more confusing. After all, she hadn't known she was possessed. And she certainly hadn't known she was possessed by not just any entity... but a dark master in training. An entity who knew just enough to influence her, and whose powers were just enough to alter her. Her experience with mirrors had led her to have a complete breakdown. She could see herself, yes, but barely. She could, in fact, only see a hint of herself, a ghost image of herself. She had gotten to the point where she thought she had died. That she was, in fact, a ghost. That she was living in a sort of ghost world. As I said, a breakdown.

It wasn't until years later that she just sort of... let it go. She quit worrying about it. She accepted it. Hell, she quit thinking about it altogether. She suspected, on some level, that she might have gone insane, but she quit worrying about that, too. She was who she was, and that was just fine. She was allowed to be a weirdo. She was allowed to even be dead, if she was, in fact, dead. After all, it had been many years now since she had even gotten sick. And didn't she heal much faster, too? She did, within days sometimes.

A part of her suspected she was a vampire. She certainly had shown traits of it. But she didn't put much thought into that either. Life was easier when she quit searching for answers. Life was easier when she just let herself be. Even if letting herself be meant that sometimes she had some very strange and erratic thoughts. Even when she got so mad sometimes that she wanted to kill someone.

But those thoughts passed, too, as they always did. And so, she had gone about her life, hating the sun, reveling in her strength, hungering for blood, shying away from mirrors, healing far too rapidly, thinking thoughts that weren't her own, looking far younger than she should, and just basically getting along, certain that she had, at some point in her life, gone completely insane. But she was okay with that, too. She was okay with all of it.

"In fact," she summed up, sitting back in my front passenger seat, her window halfway down, her face toward the sun, "I kind of like who I am. I mean, it's fun and all. I like being different. I like being stronger than most guys. I like it all. Except for maybe the mirror part. I still can't really get used to that. I mean, what is that about?"

"I think I know," I said.

"You do?" she asked. "Truthfully, I haven't talked about any of this in years. Maybe ten years. Maybe longer. I don't even know why I'm talking about it to you now."

"I know that, too."

She looked at me sideways. "What's going on, Samantha?"

"The sun..." I began. "Is it bothering you now?"

She blinked at me, then looked out her side window—and directly up at the sun. She squinted, and I saw the first real signs of minor crow's feet spreading from the corners of her eyes. I was certain those fine lines hadn't been there just a few minutes earlier.

"No," she said, shaking her head slowly. "No, it doesn't."

Then she looked down at her hands. I saw it, too. Her nails, which had been thicker than most—but not as thick and pointy as my own—had shrunk to a very normal size. They looked normal, in fact. The backs of her hands, I also noted, were not quite as smooth as they had been. The skin buckled and raised a little, just like my sister's did, just like everyone's did in their mid-to-late thirties and early forties. Everyone, that is, but people like us.

Although now... yes, now, she was not one of *us,* was she?

"What's happening, Sam?" she asked, sitting up and pulling down the sun visor and flipping open the hidden mirror there. And as she checked herself, touching her face and opening her eyes and mouth, the color drained from her face.

She flipped the visor back up and took a deep, deep breath. Something we hadn't discussed: her breathing had probably slowed, too. Now, she was forced to take in more air, forced to use somewhat dormant lungs, which she was doing now, like a babe breathing for the first time.

"My breathing... my lungs..." she gasped, taking more air. "There's something wrong with me..."

I reached out and calmed her mind, but it took a number of suggestions before she finally did calm down. Now, she was breathing easier, although not quite normally. The very act seemed a little foreign to her. Her nostrils flared and her cheeks puffed. Her chest, rising and falling, sometimes shuddered with the effort.

"It's gone, Sam. Whatever I had, is gone."

"I know," I said.

She rolled her head toward me, nostrils flared, still fighting for breath—or, rather, struggling to control her breathing. "You know what happened to me, don't you?"

"I do," I said.

"Tell me!" she said, her eyes flashing with anger. "Tell me everything."

Chapter 10

I was in Jacky's gym, doing real damage to both the punching bag and Jacky himself.

No, I didn't enjoy hurting Jacky, but the little bugger seemed to, I dunno, like it or something. He kept hanging in there, kept holding that bag steady, even as I pounded it into mush. Granted, the sun was not yet down, and so, the bag—and Jacky— were mostly spared. But once it descended... all bets were off. One clean punch might just send Jacky and the bag flying across the gym.

It was after school, and, for once, I actually believed Tammy was home studying. Her near-miss with death last year had prompted her to take life a little more seriously, and to recognize that bad decisions often led to bad results. Granted, the runaway big rig that had nearly stolen my baby girl from me wasn't her fault, but she most certainly should not have been drinking and out that late, with a new set of friends she barely knew and could not trust.

She saw the light, so to speak. Granted, that didn't stop the continuous eye rolls or the "whatevers" or any other sound or gesture that was cleverly designed by teenagers the world over to remind mothers that we were super lame and that we "just didn't get them."

Still, she was keeping better hours and working harder in school and being a little more picky with her friends. Honestly, was there anything more a mother of a teenage daughter could ask? Oh, and perhaps the biggest change of all: she had decided to take a break from dating boys.

Music to my freakin' ears.

Now, halfway across the gym and in one of the sparring rings, Anthony was circling a full-grown man. Both had gloves on, and both were displaying perfect footwork. I knew about such footwork, having now been trained by the best, Jacky.

And once Jacky had understood that my son was, well, different—very, very different—he put the brakes on Anthony's fast-track to boxing stardom. Yeah, it had been time to let Jacky in on a family secret, and, so far, the old Irishman seemed to be handling it well. No weird sidelong glances. No weird questions. No ridiculous fear of us. Then again, I could never, ever imagine Jacky being afraid of anything.

But once it had been understood that my son

had an unfair advantage, Jacky understood that my boy should never be allowed to box mere mortals in competition. Instead, Jacky had taken to using my son to train his mortal protégés, so to speak. It was understood by Jacky's young boxing studs that if they could last a round with my thirteen-year-old boy, then they, the boxers, were clearly on their way up.

Now, as I glanced into the ring, I suspected this young mortal boxer—who was about twenty, maybe—was clearly *not* on his way up. Even with head gear on, he staggered about the ring as my son landed punch after punch. Anthony stepped back and let the guy regain his balance. This was practice after all. Not a death match.

As for me, I wasn't done with the heavy bag yet. I needed to hit something, and I needed to hit something hard and often, as I worked out what the devil I was dealing with. Which was exactly the problem.

I was dealing with the devil.

And while I punched, I relived the last few moments I'd had with Sandy Damayanti. She had wanted to hear it all, except I didn't think she was ready to hear it all. In fact, I was pretty damn sure she wasn't ready to hear any of it.

Turned out, she *liked* being a partial vampire, even if she didn't know she was a partial vampire. There was a lot to like, admittedly. The problem was, she was providing a safe house to the entity within, an entity whose time had run out. The devil and his three-headed dog had found them, and they were going to drag him down to hell, even if it meant killing her in the process.

She didn't deserve to die. She was just someone who had recklessly played with an Ouija board—someone who had inadvertently opened herself up to an entity on the run. No doubt, a case of bad timing. As in wrong place, wrong time.

That Sandy had darker tendencies was a different story. In the end, she didn't mind being different. She also didn't seem to mind the darkness within her, which helped me to understand how some vampires seemed to easily co-exist with the entities possessing them.

They enjoyed hosting the dark entities, I realized, as I circled the bag, punching with a flurry of jabs. Jacky circled with me, keeping the bag between him and me. Not all who become vampires were good people. Had I been a good person? I liked to think I was. I was certainly the best wife I could have been. The best federal agent I could have been, putting the bad guys behind bars. And certainly, the best mother I could be, then and still.

Obviously, some people leaned toward the darkness. Some people bonded with the darkness. Some people reveled in the darkness.

Sandy had been such a person. She and her entity had been a match made in heaven. Or hell.

Or *because* of hell.

As I sat with her in the minivan, as she waited for my answer—and growing impatient, frustrated and scared—I had weighed my choices. I could tell her that I had removed the entity within her, an entity she honestly hadn't minded hosting, the entity that had been the source of her considerable power (even if her power was far less than a full vampire). She might or might not believe my story about the devil coming for her. More than likely, she would resent me. More than likely, she might become suicidal. To lose so much power was to lose, well, her identity. I decided to take the easy way out, which might or might not bite me in the ass later.

Although there was no way I could replace a lifetime of memories that featured her unusual gifts and talents and curses, I could alter how she *perceived* them.

So, I had given her some not-so-subtle suggestions, planted deep in her subconscious, that she was better off being free of the entity, that she was normal again, healthy again, happy again. Now, she could lead a normal life. Of course, I wrapped a lot of good feeling around the word "normal," knowing her predilection for the macabre. How long such suggestions held, I didn't know. I suspected for a while. Perhaps a long while. What would happen if and when they wore off? Well, she wouldn't be a happy camper. That I knew.

Once done, I sent her off, hoping like hell that I hadn't just created the world's next super-villain.

Or my own next great enemy.

***

We took a break, and I watched Jacky stagger over and collapse into a ringside chair. There, he kept an eye on his latest protégé, a young Mexican kid who seemed faster than greased lightning. That is, until he sparred with my own son.

I took a seat on a rolled mat, wiping my considerable sweat with a towel of suspect cleanliness. Then again, what did I care about germs or even diseases? I could come down with the worst case of bubonic plague, only to watch it disappear before my very eyes.

I shook my head and marveled again at the powerful dark magicks that fueled my body. *You were messing with some dark juju, Elizabeth.*

It was, I think, the first time I had spoken to her directly in a long, long time. Speaking to her directly seemed to give her the wherewithal to rise up from my consciousness and acknowledge my words. Perhaps, permission was the better word. Either way, I heard the words, clear as a bell, even if whispered from seemingly a great distance away:

You have no idea, Sssamantha...

I shrugged. She was probably right. What the hell did I know of black magic—or whatever it was that Elizabeth and the other highly evolved dark masters practiced? Maybe it was their own form of magic. Maybe they had inadvertently tapped into something very powerful and dark, something that existed beyond even heaven and hell.

And I was presently hosting one of the

strongest of them all.

Grrreat, I thought, and sipped from my water bottle.

How all of this didn't end badly for me someday, I didn't know. I mean, surely there was going to be some great, epic battle in my future, a battle in which I would be forced to stare down a legion of dark masters, perhaps with the alchemist and his army of Light Warriors by my side—an army that had already made it known it wished to recruit my son.

My son...

Who was presently dancing around the boxing ring with footwork that Floyd Mayweather, Jr. would die for. The young Mexican boxer, maybe twenty years old, did all he could to get a bead on Anthony. My son was wearing a tank top that did little to hide his already-impressive physique, a physique that was only getting more muscular as the months progressed. And not just muscular but... thicker. His shoulders were broadening. His chest was expanding. He was already five feet, eleven inches tall, with no sign of slowing down. Now, as I watched from the shadows, as he danced smoothly around the ring, I could have been watching a full-grown man, a professional, himself teaching the up-and-coming fighter. But that wasn't the case, was it? The Hispanic fighter had seven years on my son.

"When it comes to your son, years matter little."

I gasped, startled. It's not easy to sneak up on

me, but someone had. And not just anyone. My ex-guardian angel, an angel who had abandoned me at my hour of greatest need, an angel who had, in fact, allowed my attack ten years ago. Perhaps even orchestrated it. After my attack had rendered me immortal, his guardian duties had been severed. Once severed, he was free to pursue another type of relationship with me, a romantic one—and one I had no interest in at all. Not now, not ever. I would never, ever forgive him for allowing my attack. He was, quite frankly, the worst guardian angel. Ever. Not exactly boyfriend material.

I said, "Well, he's still my son, and he's only thirteen, and just last night, I watched him smell his own armpits... and he seemed to enjoy it. Lord help me, he seemed to enjoy it. So, in case I have to spell it out for you, he's just a kid, a boy, a teenage boy, despite the fact that he could probably beat you to smithereens."

I doubted it, but it felt good saying it.

He didn't defend himself, or feel a need to correct me. He just stared at me. Stared and stared and stared. So creepy, but also kind of exciting, too. Terrible at his job or not, he was still beautiful to behold. Too beautiful. I noted there was no impression in the tightly rolled mat where he sat, whereas my own booty put quite a dent in it. I wasn't sure how I felt about the dent differential.

"I am invisible, Sam. More so, I am without body."

Despite my residual anger for him, I was

always fascinated by the beautiful bastard. "Are you always invisible?"

"Usually, Sam."

"Can you take a body when you need to?"

"I can manifest a body, yes."

"You don't need to possess the living?" I said. I noted that my inner alarm remained quiet, dormant, content, at peace. All of which was good news to me.

"Never, Sam."

Angel magic—or whatever it was called—was certainly beyond my own experience. To be able to manifest a corporeal, physical body from thin air seemed a true miracle.

"We are all miracles, Sam."

"Thank you for that, Deepak," I said.

Ishmael cocked his head to one side, no doubt probing my brain for the reference. He seemed to find it, and nodded without comment. My ex-guardian angel was a big fellow. He was, by my estimates, exactly twice as big as me, maybe bigger. Of course, this was his non-physical form. I had no idea if his physical form would be just as big. I had seen him many times now, and each time, I had only seen his energetic form. He wore a suggestion of what might have been a robe or a tunic. His was a mottled gray. He wore no shoes, and his feet were big ol' honkers. His hands were clasped together in his lap. A sort of soft wind seemed to emanate from him, which I didn't understand at all. It was as if he powered his own solar windstorm.

"You are close, Sam Moon. And as always, your intuitiveness is remarkable."

"Remarkable, how?" I asked. And, hey, if I was getting a compliment, I at least wanted to know why the hell I was so amazing and what I'd inadvertently intuited.

He waited for me to catch up, and, my mind being what it was, I played over my last sentence. And then, it hit me, and it hit me hard. "The sun," I said.

"Yes, Sam."

"You are the sun." My words startled me. Never in my life had I ever expected to utter them, but here they were, pouring out of me, and they felt... right.

He said nothing, only cocked his head a little more, and now I saw his wavy, brown hair lift and fall, his bangs blowing a little more, the hem of his tunic-thing ruffling. I felt the wind, too, and I was certain, damn certain, it was coming off of him. And now, I felt the heat, too. A mild heat. But I could feel it, and it was coming off him in waves.

"We are forged in the fires of the sun, Samantha Moon, just as other entities of your world are forged in the heart of Mother Earth."

"The in-betweeners," I said.

"I know your reference, but it is not accurate. These entities are natural, rather than unnatural, forged with love, rather than hate, confusion, desperation or ego."

"Who are they?" I asked.

"They are the true earth angels, but they are not ready to show themselves to you, Sam."

"My daughter says she's seen them..."

"And so, she has."

"Is it because I am what I am... that they don't show themselves to me?"

But the angel didn't respond; instead, he sat there, emitting heat and a gentle solar breeze. I could almost hear Anthony now: "I emit wind and heat, too, Ma!"

"Your son is amusing," said Ishmael. "You have captured his spirit perfectly."

"You mean I have captured his guy humor perfectly. I think, officially, one hundred percent of all males like fart humor."

The angel next to me cocked his head a little, and smiled. He didn't understand the statement, which was fine.

"Let's get back to this sun business... do you live in the sun?"

"We can return to the sun, Sam. Mostly, I find myself here, on Earth, watching over your own son."

He didn't say any more, or hint that there was more to say, but I suspected there was something further he wanted to add. I had no sense of his mind, although I knew he was deep within my own.

"You are correct, Sam. I am here to give you news."

"Then give it."

He paused, then said, "I am here to inform you

that my services are no longer needed."

"Come again?"

"Your son is perfectly capable of taking care of himself."

"My son is only thirteen."

"Your son possesses talents that even I can't match, Sam."

I opened my mouth to protest. But then, closed it again.

Ishmael went on. "Anthony is an anomaly on this planet, Samantha Moon. Although it's too soon to tell, I have reason to believe he is an immortal."

"And you know this how?" I asked.

"I have seen low-level toxins get destroyed in his bloodstream at an atomic level. I have seen the strength of his heart, and it is a strong heart indeed, Sam. As strong as I have ever seen. I have seen his cells regenerate at a phenomenal rate. All of which are indicators of..." He let his voice trail off, and I sensed his hesitancy.

"Immortality?" I said.

"Perhaps, Sam. Or perhaps something else. Perhaps something closer to the werewolves of your world, or the Lichtenstein monsters, of which you are acquainted now. Each has a prolonged lifespan."

"But not quite immortal," I said.

He nodded. "Additionally, his strength has grown considerably since the years I've been watching over him. It is obvious he needs no further assistance."

"But—and I can't emphasize this enough—he's

only thirteen."

"Within your son lies a great warrior, Sam."

I opened my mouth to protest some more, but then closed it again. I wasn't going to beg Ishmael to watch my son. And I wasn't going to tell him about the terrible premonitions I'd been having about my son. Except vampires were not known for premonitions—or, rather, I wasn't known for them, outside of the occasional prophetic dream. This was no dream. Just a feeling in my gut. A feeling I hated. But maybe these were just natural feelings a mother had for her kids. Except I hadn't been 'natural' in eleven years. Was it a mother's instincts or a psychic hit? I didn't know.

"Your son can take care of himself, Sam. You need not fear."

"So, what then?" I asked. "You're going to go on your merry way? Back into the sun, or wherever the fuck you came from?"

I was surprised by my own vitriol. Yes, the bastard had sold me out, thrown me under the bus, but he'd done it for love, apparently; and, ultimately, I couldn't hold it against him. At least, not for all eternity. Look at me, forgiving the very entity who got me into this mess.

Ishmael didn't reply. He sat and emanated warmth and a wind and, dammit, a gentle peace. Still, his silence was telling. I said, "You're no longer welcomed home, are you?"

His head cocked a little to one side. "Your perception is on target again, Sam Moon."

"You haven't been welcomed since you abandoned your, ah, post," I said, not knowing a better word.

"My charge," he said. "My human."

"Seems a harsh penalty," I said. "Exile."

The energy flowing from him seemed to pick up a little. I watched my own bangs rise and fall on the supernatural solar winds.

He did not move or blink. He did not gesture in any way with his hands, head, or body. His presence next to me was vastly... alien. Even the creepiest vampires—and ghosts, for that matter—seemed to exude a *humanness*. Something to indicate they had, at least at some point in time, been human. Even the devil had his strange, strange smile. Even the devil blinked because, well, his human host needed to blink. His host's humanness came through, whether the devil wanted it to or not. But the entity before me—the fallen angel before me—gave off none of that. He gave off, if anything, a strange, comforting warmth that seemed both foreign and deeply personal. Then again, if he was from the sun, then that made him the very definition of an alien. And being my former guardian angel probably explained the comfort part.

"This is weird," I summed up.

"Perhaps, Sam. But let's be clear: I am not a fallen angel. You had it right the first time: I am an exiled angel."

"Because fallen angels choose darkness," I said.

"Yes, Sam."

"And become demons," I added.

"It is a misunderstood word... but, yes."

"Misunderstood, how?"

"The connotation suggests that demons are mindless entities of pure evil, commanded by the devil alone."

"This is not the case?"

"They are not so different from me, Sam."

"They can think, choose, reason?"

"Yes. And calculate. They choose the dark path, and they continue to choose. At least some."

"What does that mean?"

"God forgives, Sam. And God welcomes back. Mostly, God understands that the world needs demons and devils, needs the darkness to contrast with the light. God understands such entities are fulfilling a role, and does not punish, and always welcomes home."

"That is a lot to take in," I said.

"It is," he said, knowing my thoughts intimately.

"You are suggesting that even angels and demons are on a sort of evolutionary path?"

"I am, Sam. It is a longer path, a different path. Our challenges are not the same as your challenges. Our connection to the Creator is different, too. As are our expectations and roles. But there is growth. And, yes, there are always forgiveness and redemption. For us, for everyone."

"Mind blown," I said, and made a small

explosion gesture at the side of my head, something I'd picked up from Anthony. Or maybe Sheldon on *The Big Bang Theory*. Love that nerdy goofball.

"And there is room for us to love," he said. "And to be loved."

"With humans?" I asked.

"Sometimes," he said. "Although it is not very common."

I was about to voice my objection to his statement—after all, look at what he'd given up just to make himself known to me—when I read a little deeper between the lines, so to speak. I said, "And it is rarer still for an angel—a guardian angel—to fall in love with his, um, charge."

He looked at me, and now I saw his eyes moving, moving, moving. They were looking at me, my face, all of my face, every inch of it. And I saw and felt his love. So much warmth... so much love...

"It is rare indeed," he finally said.

"And to be loved by one's own guardian angel..."

"Is the rarest of all."

"Because one generally never meets one's own guardian angel," I said.

"It takes, as you can imagine, extenuating circumstances to make it so."

"Like making me immortal."

"*Allowing* you to be immortal," he corrected. "But, yes, Sam. And I hope, someday, you can forgive me for allowing it to be."

His words were dull, flat, lifeless. The angel

Ishmael spoke frankly, with little or no innuendo, with little or no humor. What you saw was what you got. Although I suspected...

"Yes, Sam. I suspect the same."

"That the more you are around me—or humans—the more human you would become?"

"Close. The more human-like. I will always be what I am."

"A creature from the sun," I said.

"Yes..."

My son was taking a break and speaking with Jacky quietly, the way they often did, with their heads together and Jacky holding the back of my son's head. It was special and sweet. I had seen it a hundred times with boxers and trainers, but seeing Jacky do it with my son... well, it gave me a thrill that was hard to put into words. It was the feeling of relief, joy, and appreciation, all rolled into one good-feeling vibe.

I looked at the angelic being next to me, an entity who had given up eternity for me, although I had never asked him to—and had never known he existed.

"I will forgive you someday," I suddenly said. "I think. But maybe not now, and maybe not any time soon."

"That is all I can ask, Samantha Moon." He paused. "There is something else on your mind."

"There is," I said, and took a big, worthless breath. "I met the devil yesterday."

"You did, Sam."

"So, he's real then?" I said.

"What do you believe?"

"I believe it to be so."

"I believe you did, too, Sam."

"Shit."

"The devil performs a role, Sam. And he does it well, but one need not fear him. After all, hell is only an illusion, a construct of the mind."

"Say that to the people suffering in it," I said.

"An illusion as well. When they are done suffering, when they have experienced what they need to experience, and what they created, they will move on to something better, something greater. They will move on to the peace they seek, the forgiveness they seek. Hell is only real... until it isn't."

"Until people stop believing," I said.

"Correct, Sam."

"Just how powerful is the devil?" I asked.

Ishmael studied me a moment longer, then answered: "As powerful as you allow him to be."

Chapter 11

"Then why don't you have that same creepy smile, too?" Allison asked.

"Because my possession isn't temporary. It is who I am."

Allison, of course, had experienced such temporary possession, having been distantly related to the Thurman clan, and thus, susceptible to the entity that haunted them. Or, rather, their bloodline.

"As in, your body accepts it more?"

"Maybe," I said. We were at Alicia's, a restaurant in Brea. "Or maybe it has to do with blood. Or, more accurately, the transfer of blood." I'd been thinking about her question, too, which is probably why she had brought up over lunch. I said, "Vampires and werewolves, as you know, are created through bites. In effect, through a physical opening into the body."

"Unlike a psychic opening."

"Right. Not to mention, the entity that possessed your family—"

"Distant family."

"Fine, yes, distant family. Anyway, the entity also seemed more demonic in nature, did it not?"

"As in, not your typical highly evolved dark master?"

"Right," I said.

"So, you're suggesting the more demonic—"

"Or more non-human," I corrected.

"The more non-human the entity, the more the body rejects it?"

I nodded. "Exactly. The less the body can accommodate it, assimilate with it."

"Which is the reason for the extreme expressions, the grinning and the frowning?"

"It's a working theory," I said, shrugging.

"Does it even matter?" asked Allison.

"Perhaps only in identifying other such entities."

She nodded. "Or the devil himself."

"Bingo," I said.

"Why does the devil even want you?" asked Allison. "I mean, why doesn't he just sic his big, bad, three-headed dog on Danny?"

"Danny—surprise, surprise—was further along in his, ah, studies than any of us could have imagined or, quite frankly, guessed."

"Which means..."

"Which means he's particularly well hidden."

"I don't understand," said Allison. "Why is the devil going after him and not, say, you? Or the thing inside you?"

"Elizabeth," I said, and I did my best to explain to Allison how dark masters—especially highly evolved dark masters—had escaped the death cycle —and slipped beyond the devil's radar.

She seemed to follow. "While mid-level masters, if that's what Danny was, haven't yet escaped the reach of the devil."

"Right," I said. "Such entities are in a sort of limbo. They know just enough to avoid the devil, but not enough to escape him—or hell— altogether." Calling Danny an entity was just... so... damn... weird.

"It's almost enough for one to seek to become a dark master," said Allison.

"That, or not buy into the concept of hell," I said. "Or lead a life that you believe will be punished later."

Allison picked at her Caesar salmon salad. And as she'd ordered, I said something to the effect of, "Say *that* three times." In which both Allison and the waitress proceeded to rattle off "Caesar salmon salad" three and even four times, until I finally waved the waitress away. Show-offs.

Now, Allison only picked at it. Me, I had no problem eating my BLT that had just the right amount of B and L and T, along with mayo and a dash of honey mustard. The homemade potato chips didn't last long either. I doubted—no, I knew—that

I derived no nutritional value from my meals. I also knew—or suspected—that my taste buds had been downgraded, so to speak. They had yet to regenerate fully. Still, even at partial capacity, I savored the crap out of my meal. Going eight years without food did wonders for an appetite. Even if my appetite was only mental, and not really physical. Emotional eating is a real thing, even for vampires.

"So, what are you going to do, Sam?" asked Allison.

Allison had already lived through most of my memories of the devil, including my encounter with the thing in Sandy. She'd seen firsthand, so to speak, how I'd excised the entity from the possessed girl, and the Devil and his minions had gathered up the lost soul, dragging him, no doubt, to his own private hell.

I said, "I was told I could save another life."

"Like you saved Sandy's?"

"Right," I said.

"And since when can the devil take a life?" asked Allison, speaking a little louder than I'd liked. Our telepathic connection had always been particularly strong, thanks to her allowing me to feed from her, a process that both enhanced her witchy skills, and nearly gave Elizabeth enough strength to burst out of me and, probably, fully take control of yours truly, maybe even forever. We'd stopped the feedings, and Elizabeth slipped back down, down, down—made irrelevant once again by a steady diet of cow and pig blood. If BLTs enhanced her strengths, then I'd really be screwed. Or coffee. Or...

"Focus, Sam," said Allison, somehow following my mental train of thought.

I said, "Can the devil kill?" I shrugged. "I don't know what the cosmic rules are—or if there are any."

"There are some rules, Sam. For instance, one such rule is that we are given free will."

"Like the free will to believe in any afterlife we choose," I said. "Even hell."

Allison shrugged and picked at her salad some more. "Or the free will to decide to do good in the world. To help, to heal, to bless."

"Sure, Pollyanna," I said. "But we're talking about in the context of the devil killing humans."

"Blech," asked Allison. "He's such a downer."

I laughed and nearly snatched her salad from her. What had once been a beautiful piece of salmon, had been ground down into flaky bits and spread thin. Terrible. Just terrible.

"Fine. Have it," she said, and pushed it toward me.

I might have felt guilty taking it; that is, until I had my first glorious bite. I ate and scanned Alicia's, the small but cute restaurant. Painted vines on the wall. Also real vines, too, which was an odd mix. A small mercantile store that sold baskets and pots and pans and books and washcloths, and everything a cute little kitchen could need.

I also spotted the redhead, sitting there in her usual spot against the wall and near the door. If anything, her hair seemed even redder than before. She sported an aura, which meant she was mortal, but she also projected something else, something that always bothered me... or at least intrigued me. It was a sense of *knowing*. As if she seemed to know who and what we were.

"She can probably see auras," said Allison. "Or lack thereof. You're probably freaking her out."

"Or she can read minds," I said. "Or possess any number of peculiar quirks and oddities."

"Or none of them," said Allison, looking over her shoulder at the redhead, who reluctantly look away and gave a half-assed effort to show some interest in a plant hanging in front of her. "Maybe we just talk too loud. And when I say we, I mean you."

I ignored my friend. "One of us needs to talk to her."

Then again, she wasn't hurting anyone. After all, Allison and I were about as weird as they came. Anyone with even a modicum of extrasensory ability was probably able to pick up some strange vibes from our table.

"Maybe you should stop thinking of yourself as strange or different, Sam. Maybe it's time to acknowledge that there is far more to this world than most mortals can see or know. Maybe you should start considering how privileged you have been to know such secrets—how honored you are to have had the inner workings of the Universe cracked open for you."

"Geez, Louise. How long have you been planning that speech?" I asked, turning my attention back to my friend—and off the mysterious redhead.

"It's been nagging at me for a while, Sam. Often you seem to refer to yourself as something less, somehow. When in fact, you are much more than most of us could ever imagine or hope for."

"Even you?" I asked.

She opened her mouth, closed it again. Speaking of closed, her mind was still blocked from my own, as it had been, ever since one her witchy friends—a ghost of all things—decided that I was closer to being the enemy than a friend. Allison, bound to her triad in ways that I might not ever know or understand, had honored the request... but only so far. She didn't cut ties with me, but she also didn't allow me to access her mind, which was a shame, because telepathy was often a whole hell of a lot easier than talking. Especially in a crowded restaurant.

"Does he call himself Satan?" asked Allison.

"I don't know. But probably. He exists, after all, because of humanity's collective consciousness, apparently. And most of us call him Satan. Or Lucifer. Personally, I think he's a fucking creep."

I might have said that last part a little too loudly. Heads snapped around, especially the pretty redhead. Did I need to talk to the redhead? No, I didn't need to. Personally, I think it's okay to let people be. To let them have their secrets. To leave well enough alone. But I suspected—oh yes, I suspected—that she and I would one day have a heart to heart.

Perhaps even soon.

"Good for you guys," said a jealous Allison, picking up on my thoughts, and not bothering to hide the hurt in her voice. "I hope you guys really hit it off."

I decided not to point out that six months earlier, she had walked out of my life—only to return shortly thereafter, not necessarily with her tail between her legs, but certainly with an apology on her lips.

I nodded. "It is, of course, perfectly logical to think that, after one meeting, she will become my new best friend."

Allison caught a subtle meaning I hadn't necessarily intended. Or rather, she'd heard what she wanted to hear. "I'm your best friend, Sam?"

I ignored her, not wanting Allison to get off the needy hook so easily. "In some countries, best friends adopt puppies together. I wonder if she likes labradoodles, too..."

"You're incorrigible, Sam Moon."

"I suspect we would be inseparable. Maybe she should just move in? I could always set her up in my office..."

"I hate you, Sam."

"No, you don't."

"No, I don't," she said. She paused, debated

what to do with her hands, then settled with folding them in front of her. "I've never had a friend like you."

"Even in your triad?"

"They..." She paused. "They are different. They are necessary. They are important, and we do good work together."

"I'm trying not to feel hurt over here," I said.

"But I choose to be your friend, Sam. I'm honored to be your friend. I'm excited to be your friend—hey, stop doing that!"

I was making gagging motions, really sticking my finger down my throat and leaning to the side. A lady sitting next to me scooted her chair back and said, "Oh dear!"

"I'm okay now," I said, and winked at Allison, and I winked at the redhead looking at me, too. The redhead blushed a little and turned back to her food and the hanging plants. Luckily, I was more interesting than a fern.

"Are you quite done?" asked Allison, turning red herself. Allison was a witch and a psychic (although the two might go hand-in-hand), but not at immortal; meaning, her bodily functions worked normally, like blood flow. My bodily functions only 'kinda' worked, and mostly they did so begrudgingly. Mostly, I operated on a supernatural level, which is a weird thing to say unless, you know, you don't have a heartbeat. Or can't see yourself in a mirror.

"We get it, Sam. You're... different. And please

never talk about my bodily functions again. Like, *eww*."

"Hey, you almost said weird."

"No, I didn't. And you can never prove it. Besides, different is a better word. We're both different. We're not less. In fact, we might even be a little more. Or a lot more."

I couldn't argue with that, especially when I'm flying over Orange County as a giant dragon or bat, or whatever the hell Talos is.

Perhaps a little of both, I heard a distant voice say.

I could be wrong here—but I was seventy-five percent sure those were Talos's words. Like in my head. From across space and time and, for all I knew, dimensions.

Crazy, I thought. *Just too damn crazy.*

"I heard it too, Sam. Not so crazy. So, that was Talos?"

Okay, now, I was ninety percent sure. "I guess so, yeah."

"He sounds... wise. You are lucky to have him."

"Oh, God. Please tell me you're not going to be jealous over a dragon, too."

"Maybe a little jealous," she said. "Who wouldn't want a dragon?"

"We're not having this conversation," I said.

"Oh, but we are, Sam. We're having it real good."

And with that, I started laughing, and I didn't

stop laughing until we had cleared out most of the restaurant. Then again, it was kind of a small place, and lunch hour was mostly over anyway.

"You never answered my question, Sam," said Allison, wiping the tears of laughter from her eyes.

"What question?"

"Are you going to find Danny for the devil?"

"Ah, that question." I took in some air, held it for far too long, then let it go. I nodded, and kept nodding as I said, "If I can save another life, then, yes."

"But how will you find him?"

I had been thinking about that all night, too, and I might have come up with an answer. As was the case with Sandy, I suspected I didn't have a lot of time. After all, the devil dog had shown up that very night, along Lemon Street. And had I not met with Sandy the very next day, I suspected she might have met an unfortunate end... all to get at the entity within her.

"I have a plan," I said. "But I'm going to need your help."

Allison brightened considerably. Her need to be needed had just been granted.

"Oh, shut up, Sam. I don't need you."

"Yes, you do."

"Fine, whatever." She rolled her eyes and did her best to look hurt, but that only lasted a fraction of a second. She leaned across the table, eyes flashing. "So, what do you need me to do?"

"I'll tell you in a minute, but first I need to call

Tammy and have her pick up her brother."

"The same brother who's, like, six inches taller than she is? And who can, like, stop a speeding train?"

"Yes, and hardly. I've been having a... feeling lately." Which wasn't like me. I rarely had psychic feelings, unless they were dream-induced. These weren't. I just didn't want Anthony left alone, not now, and not with his guardian angel now off the case. My guardian angel, no less. My ex-guardian angel. I knew Allison had caught most of that.

"I did, Sam. And I kind of wish I hadn't. I'm pretty sure you just gave me a headache."

"Sorry," I said.

"How long have you been having these psychic hits?"

"Maybe a week, maybe longer."

"And what do they entail?"

"Something to do with Anthony," I said. "Something about not leaving him alone."

"But isn't that every parent's fear?"

I shrugged, suddenly miserable. "Probably. But not every parent has a child who's a beacon to every supernatural creep out there."

Allison knew about the silver serpent that ran through my son's aura, a serpent that marked him as a potential Light Warrior. Marked him for the good guys... and for the bad guys, too. "You can't protect your kids all of the time, Sam. Ishmael did say your son would be okay."

"I'd rather not take the word of a very bad

guardian angel," I snapped.

I pulled out my cell phone and called Tammy. She picked up on the last possible ring, to remind me of my place in her life. I reminded her of her place, too, which was being a big sister. She didn't like where this was going and put up a fight, and before we hung up, I counted three "I hate yous" and seven "whatevers." Most important, she had agreed to pick up her brother. I said, "I love you," and she said, "Whatever." Okay, eight.

I turned to Allison. "Okay, let's go."

Chapter 12

Anthony knew he wasn't like other kids.

He also knew that he wasn't like other people. Heck, no one in his family was. Even his dad had started acting strangely at the end. Anthony was certain that Mommy hadn't seen it; in fact, she had been so busy being mad at Daddy, that she didn't see him changing before her eyes.

Anthony didn't know all the details of what Daddy was up to, but Tammy had filled him in later. Daddy, apparently, owned and operated a strip club, where women were paid to get naked—a thought that intrigued Anthony to no end. Why Daddy would do that, Anthony didn't know. He also didn't care too much, one way or another. To his young thirteen-year-old mind, his daddy could do little wrong, and running a strip club didn't seem like the worst thing ever, at least to a teenage boy.

It was after school, and Anthony found himself alone in the pick-up area, a spot in front of the school. He was in eighth grade, and was the second tallest boy in school. Anthony was only one inch shorter than Phillip McGarry, and that was all right by him. Anthony already had the reputation for being a big weirdo. He didn't need to be a weirdo and the tallest boy in school, too! That would be just too much. Or so he thought.

Most boys walked to school, or took the bus, but Mommy still liked picking him up, and so he let her. Walking would be a drag. It was, like, twenty miles away (although he had heard his mom say it was only four miles away). Still, four miles seemed like forever! Better to have Mommy pick him up. He knew he had to quit calling her Mommy, and quit calling his dad "Daddy." He didn't understand why he still thought of them as Mommy and Daddy. When his dad died, something inside Anthony sort of died, too. He could feel it. Or maybe it hadn't so much died as stunted him on the inside. Certainly not on the outside! But inside, he still felt like a little boy who missed his daddy, and he couldn't get past that feeling, no matter how hard he tried. And if calling his parents Mommy and Daddy felt right, then so be it—although he would never, ever use the names around his friends; that is, what few friends he had.

One or two of the boys in school seemed to not mind so much if they ate lunch together, but mostly, kids stayed away from him. They had heard that he was freakishly strong. A number of them had challenged him, wanting to fight him, but he had ignored them for the most part. One boy who wouldn't let up, kept getting in Anthony's face, day after day, saying terrible things about him and his sister and mother. He was a boy Anthony didn't know, a one-time big shot from elementary school who was still trying to be a big shot in middle school.

As so, he had tripped Anthony one day. The foot had shot out from behind a door, but Anthony, instead of falling, had gracefully found his footing again. But in the process of regaining his balance, he had swung an arm out at the tripper. The shaggy blond-haired kid had slammed into the lockers so hard that he had blacked out. Anthony had even caught him before the wannabe bully had hit the ground. In fact, Anthony had carried him to the nurse's office over a shoulder.

Now, no one messed with him, although he saw groups of boys conspiring against him as he passed. He heard his name whispered, with both awe and hate. Anthony suspected they were going to jump him someday and try to beat the strangeness out of him—and maybe he would let them, if just to appear normal. But Anthony knew himself. He knew that, once attacked, something triggered inside him, and he would fight back, often too hard, and often hurting the other boys. If only they would just leave him be.

Mostly, they did.

Anthony had long since discovered that playing sports with the other boys wasn't much fun at all. He was better than them. A lot better. So much so that it was kinda freaky. Sure, the coaches here at Jenkins Middle School had pestered him nearly nonstop to join basketball and track and field, but Anthony had always politely declined.

Truthfully, he only felt comfortable in Jacky's gym, working out with the old trainer, or sparring with adults, some of whom even were able to challenge Anthony, although mostly he could beat them pretty easily, too. Anthony enjoyed the footwork, the give and take of punching, the dance of it all. It appealed to him on many levels, even if Anthony had to mostly hold back.

And he liked Jacky a lot. A whole lot. Jacky felt just like a grandpa to him, and Anthony really liked that feeling. He only had one living grandpa, and he lived in Vegas, and his grandparents mostly stayed there. They weren't very good grandparents, as far as Anthony was concerned, although Mommy seemed to be talking to them more and more these days on the phone.

They think we're weird, too, he thought. *Everyone, everywhere thinks we're weird.*

Mommy had talked about a special school for him, a school for kids who were different, as she said. These days, Anthony had been thinking about that school—a lot. He had almost forgotten what it was like to just be one of the boys, just another kid playing. All focus and all attention seemed to be on him all the time, but almost never in a good way. Yes, one or two girls seemed interested, and he had even spent time with them last year, but each one had eventually quit coming around. And he knew why, too. One girl had mentioned that she was being teased for hanging out with him. She even let slip what his nickname was. Man-child.

Because he was bigger than most. Maybe not the tallest, but the fullest, biggest, and clearly the strongest. His shoulders were wider, and his whiskers were filling out. Yes, whiskers. A true man-child.

He knew he was a freak. He also knew he probably would have died years ago if his mother— the queen freak herself—hadn't saved him in her own weird way. Yes, she had told him everything, and he was glad that she had. After all, he would never, ever have been able to understand what was happening to him, if she hadn't told him.

Some of his other so-called friends called him "X-man." Not just an X-men mutant, like Wolverine or Magneto, but X-man. "Hey, X-man..." they would begin. Anthony had to admit, he kind of liked it. He'd never thought of himself as a superhero before—and for all he knew, he wouldn't get any stronger than he already was. The thing is, even at thirteen, he was still stronger and faster and quicker than most adult men. He knew this, because he was able to beat just about everyone at Jacky's Gym. Unbeaten pros, too.

Unbeaten, that is, until they sparred with him.

Anthony kicked a small rock across the sidewalk. It hit a soda can in the weeds. He had been aiming at the soda can. He checked his cell phone. Mom was a little late. Again.

Luckily here, at the middle school, the principal didn't seem to care so much if parents were late. Still, they just didn't like kids milling around the school, after classes. Luckily, the principal seemed to like Anthony. Most adults seemed to like Anthony. He figured that most adults saw him as just that: an adult.

Nope, he thought. *Only thirteen. And proud of it!*

He sighed and looked into the sky. Despite being the middle of the afternoon, he saw something that he'd been seeing more and more of lately, something that could only be described as squirmy, super-bright... worms. They moved really fast though—often zig-zagging across the sky—they moved in a sort of flowing pattern. The other night, while he'd been lying in bed, he had seen the same electrified worms (as he came to think of them). Only, these electrified worms had somehow lit up his entire room. When he quit focusing on them, the room went dark again.

I can see in the dark, he had thought. But the squiggly light seemed to come only randomly, and not really enough to see too much of the room. Still, they did seem to be appearing to him more and more, which he thought was interesting.

He kicked another rock and sent it rocketing up

and over the nearby bushes, to tumble and roll across the parking lot. He thought of the words 'rock' and 'rocket,' and wondered if they were similar for a reason, but he couldn't find anything similar about a stupid pebble and a spaceship.

Now, for the first time in his life, he heard something unusual: a slight pinging sound just inside his right inner ear. Anthony shook his head and swatted near his head. Had it been a bee? A fly? Something buzzing around his head?

He didn't know. Then again, bees didn't *ping*, like sonar. They buzzed. Flies sort of hummed. A mosquito maybe? In Southern California, mosquitoes weren't very common, and Anthony didn't know much about them, but he figured, yes, it was probably a mosquito, or something like it.

Except...

The pinging came again, and again. And, no, it wasn't going on outside his head, either. It was, he was certain, happening inside his head. Maybe just inside his ear, as if something was trapped just on the other side of his eardrum.

It came again, and again, steadily louder, and steadily more persistent.

Anthony decided he didn't like the sound. Didn't like it one bit. It made him feel... uneasy. So, he tried to distract himself.

He thought again of his growing list of talents. Heck, he'd spent his last four or five years getting stronger, faster, and, well, better at just about everything. Still, kicking the small, irregular rock with perfect aim was a new one to him, so he proceeded to kick a few more, with increasing exactness. The can. A sign. A car's tire.

Which is why he didn't notice the black van pull into the school parking lot...

His phone vibrated and he looked down at it: *Mom flaked again so I'm picking you up, butthead. Almost there. And no staring at my friends. Or their boobs. They already think you are like the biggest creep.*

Yes, walking home was a bummer. But walking home with Tammy's pretty friends was a completely different story!

He was so excited that he aimed the next rock up and over the big, black van that had stopped in front of him.

A van whose back doors swung open...

Chapter 13

We were in my minivan.

"Are you sure you don't want to rent a motel room or something?" asked Allison.

"Are you propositioning me?" I asked. But as she opened her mouth to protest, I said, "I just need somewhere to lie down, okay? Relax. The front seat is as good a place as any."

The windows were cracked and we were parked in the considerable shade behind Alicia's, itself anchoring one corner of a sprawling business complex. The opposite of a cute shopping center, it was an industrial business park, with rows of single-story, cement tilt-ups that sported long rows of gritty buildings. Not a place where one would expect to find North Orange County's cutest cafe.

We found ourselves wedged between a Dumpster and a roof-access ladder, as a small wind made its way through the van. I considered letting the car idle to run the A/C, until I considered the price of gas.

"I'm fine, Sam," said Allison, blotting her forehead with the back of her hand. "Let's just get this going."

"Something wrong?" I asked.

She shrugged. "I'm just, I dunno, getting a weird feeling."

My own inner alarm was blissfully quiet. "Are we in danger?"

Allison shook her head. "I don't think it's us."

Allison's hits came and went, with varying degrees of accuracy and details. This was looking like a vague hit, and we would worry about it later. I had work to do. Or sleep to do. Or whatever the hell it is I do.

I said as much, and she replied with: "And you're sure this is the person you want to speak with? I mean, you have a whole phonebook of weirdos—myself included—and this is who you want to talk to?"

"It feels right," I said. "What can I say?"

She shrugged. "Your van is kind of cozy. I never realized how comfortable your seats are—"

"No sleeping for you," I said.

"I know, I know. I'm just getting comfort—"

"No getting comfortable for you, either. You are to wake me..."

Except, I didn't know how long I needed to be asleep. I sensed not very long, but I tried to calculate how much time Elizabeth would need. I nodded to myself, shrugged, and said, "You are to wake me in a half hour."

"And I'm just supposed to, what, sit here and do nothing for a half hour?"

"Yes," I said. "Or you can practice your spells or something. Just don't blow up the minivan. Only one of us is immortal, and it's not you."

"Very funny, Sam." She pulled up her feet and sat cross-legged in the passenger seat. She pulled out her cell phone and brought up the timer. "You need, say, a five-minute buffer to fall asleep?"

I shook my head. Already, I was feeling the heaviness come over me.

Until the sun went down, I always wanted to sleep. Falling asleep here, in the minivan, wouldn't be a problem.

Now, as I nestled deeper into the driver's seat, I sought out Elizabeth, who I knew was always there, waiting.

***

I didn't know if she would help, but I suspected she would. I suspected she wanted to be a part of my life, wanted to be needed, rather than relegated to the deepest reaches of my mind.

I had given her clear instructions, rather than a request. I didn't want to owe her anything. We weren't bargaining, not now or ever. She could help me or not. If she chose not to, then I would be less inclined to allow her to see the light of day. Simple as that.

Unfortunately for her, I feared what she would do if given too much leeway. I suspected it wouldn't take much at all for her to overwhelm my defenses, and take me over completely.

I felt myself slipping into the darkness, and, consequently, felt her rising to the surface. I'd learned not too long ago that when I'm comatose—as in sleeping—she is set free. But not in our world, no. Into another dimension. Perhaps even an alternate world.

Disembodied, she was free to roam... and to meet others of her kind, other highly evolved dark masters. It was because of this that I was no longer given access to Allison's mind. After all, Allison and her fellow witches were waging a secret war against such highly evolved dark masters. It was in everyone's best interest that I knew as little as possible about Allison's plans. Because if I knew, Elizabeth knew.

Going to sleep was easy. Heck, I needed only to *allow* myself to sleep, to give myself permission to slip away. Since I'd gotten my ring that allowed me to walk in daylight, these days, I almost never gave myself permission to sleep during the day. But now, with the windows cracked and a small breeze working its way through the van's interior, I felt myself slipping away.

Slipping far, far away...

Crazy... ass... shit, I thought, and felt the sleep

finally overwhelm me, just as Elizabeth threw open the floodgates, so to speak, and rushed up and out...

Chapter 14

There were five of them, all wearing bandanas, each looking bigger than the next. One was carrying a crossbow.

A crossbow!

The pinging in his ear was loud enough to drive him crazy. Anthony nearly ran, but he didn't. He was only thirteen—and wasn't sure what to do, despite his instincts that told him to *run.*

But he froze, and as the men surrounded him, another set of instincts kicked in.

Instincts that told him to fight.

And fight like hell.

***

As always, I have a very brief glimpse of light. It is in the far distance, and it wavers and sparkles and seems to emanate love and happiness. But the space between me and it is too vast. It might as well be a million miles away. Trillions of light years away, like a distant, unreachable star. One thing is certain: the light is not meant for me. Not now, not ever.

The light fades, as it always does, and soon, I find myself in complete and total darkness.

Emptiness.

No light, no sound, no people, no sense of up and down. No thought. No personality. No sense of self...

And here I wait silently...

Drifting and existing...

***

They surrounded him before Anthony had had time to understand what was happening, and certainly before he'd had time to run.

Somewhere, not very far away, he heard a girl scream. Then, another girl. And further away, deeper in the near-empty school, he heard a man shout, too. He recognized the man. It was the school principal. And now, Anthony heard running, too. Clumsy running. The principal was a big man.

The teacher on duty, the strict English teacher that Anthony had never really liked, rushed up to the first of the hooded men—Anthony would forever be grateful for her bravery. She'd barely gotten a word out when one of them swiped at her, raking a huge hand over her wrinkly face, sending the elderly, brave woman spinning backward. She landed in a heap on the hot cement.

Anthony started to run to her aid, but another masked man stepped before him, cutting him off. For the first time in a long, long time, Anthony felt fear. Then again, he reasoned, five masked men and a crossbow could do that to you. Especially five giant men.

Anthony wasn't very good at seeing auras, not the way his mom described them. But Anthony could see the faintest hints of them around most people. No, not around Mommy or Kingsley, but most people sported some sort of unearthly light around their bodies.

But not these five guys. Nope. They were aura-less, which meant they were like Mommy or Kingsley. They were immortal—

Wait. The fifth guy, huddled just inside the van's open back door, had an aura. He was also much smaller than the others. He was, Anthony was certain, human. Or mortal. Or whatever. He wasn't sure what the difference was.

Either way, the man sported a greenish aura—a color Anthony rarely saw these days. His math teacher sported a similar aura. His math teacher was also about the same size...

The five men cautiously circled Anthony. Very, very cautiously.

They know about me, he thought. *They know what I am. But how? Who are they?*

His mom had told him that his own aura was special, that it boasted a silver serpent that others could see. Had Anthony been fully like his mom—a true vampire—they wouldn't see it. But Anthony wasn't fully like his mom. He was sort of an in-between. He had the best of both worlds, she always told him. Unfortunately, that meant his own aura wasn't masked. That he was, as she had put it to him once, a beacon to those who might want to do him harm.

But who were these men? How had they found him?

But before he could try to puzzle it out, something flashed and Anthony instinctively spun. An arrow from the crossbow skidded off the cement behind him, clanging loudly against the chain-link fence behind him.

And now, Anthony was moving, sprinting forward, running low to the ground, going first for the man with the crossbow—just as the man reached back and pulled free another arrow...

***

I am dead, and I am alive...
Vast and contained...
Everywhere and nowhere...
Full and empty...
I am the space between stars...
I am the stars...

***

Anthony didn't know much about crossbows, other than what he'd seen in video games and TV shows. But he knew how bows and arrows worked and there was no way he was going to give the guy time to nock another arrow.

The shooter seemed aware that his time had run out, and swung the weapon around on a back sling. Instead, he brandished the crossbow arrow like a knife. A silver-tipped knife. He knew his mother had a big problem with silver, although Anthony had never seemed bothered by the metal. But these others—these massive, hooded men—seemed to think otherwise. Either way, Anthony wasn't taking any chances. Besides, a crossbow arrow would hurt like hell, no matter what.

The silver-tipped arrow came up.

Anthony knew that the best defense against knife-fighting—or, in this case, silver-tipped arrow fighting—was speed, and he had a lot of speed in him. Thanks to a trainer Jacky had brought in not too long ago—a trainer his mother didn't know about—Anthony had been taught hand-to-hand fighting. The man, Anthony would later learn, had trained Navy SEALS. Anthony also worked out with the gym's kickboxing instructor, a man with a third-degree black belt in tae kwon do. A man whose skills Anthony had quickly surpassed.

Behind the hood, the attacker's eyes widened with anticipation—eyes that had an oddly yellow hue around the iris. Eyes that looked very much like Kingsley's eyes. This man, though massive, was still clearly smaller than his mother's boyfriend, by many inches, in fact.

"Speed and displacement," he heard the trainer's voice again in his head. Anthony had not needed years of training. He often needed weeks, sometimes days or even hours. Hand-to-hand knife fighting had come naturally to him. Easily, in fact.

The arrow flashed. The man lunged, and Anthony slipped to the side. Now, the silver tip came up from the man's hip, in a motion that would have plunged it deep into Anthony's stomach.

Speed and displacement...

Anthony's arm swung down, forearm meeting forearm. The pain of bone hitting bone was ignored. The man was much bigger, and probably stronger, and Anthony had never fought for his life, but his training was true, and his instincts were truer still.

He knew that merely blocking the pointed weapon wouldn't be enough. He knew the attacker would also fight like a cornered wildcat.

Or a cornered hellhound...

A wolf, perhaps.

Almost immediately, the blocked arm swung up—and now, Anthony was really moving.

Speed and displacement...

The speed part was easy. Most people, with correct training, could block the initial knife thrust. It was the second and third thrust that usually did them in.

With displacement, one's body was no longer in one's attacker's line of sight. And now, Anthony was moving to the side, catching hold of the attacker's upthrust forearm, a thrust that would have driven the blade deep into Anthony's neck.

But Anthony was already pulling the man's arm behind him and away. A quick jerk freed the arrow from the man's grasp, and from the man who cried out. What Anthony did next was the only thing he could think of, the only thing he had been trained to do. He lowered his bent elbow straight down to the back of the man's arm, breaking his attacker's own elbow instantly in a thunderous explosion of shattering bone.

The man screamed and crumpled to a knee, and Anthony gave him a roundhouse, open-hand palm blow that should knock the guy out cold and possibly rupture the eardrum.

Whether it did or not, Anthony didn't know. Once the man went down, hands grabbed his shoulders, and Anthony, in turn, grabbed the hand and twisted as hard as he could. Fingers and wrists snapped. And now, Anthony was on his feet, turning and facing his attackers. Three were left, he knew, including his math teacher.

His math teacher!

A man who seemed to show an interest in Anthony. A man who, after class, often asked Anthony a lot of questions. Too many questions. Questions about his mom. Questions about his sister. Questions about where he lived.

I'm an idiot, Anthony thought. *An idiot.*

Another hooded giant swung a backhand at Anthony, a blow that would have surely laid out any man, let alone a thirteen-year-old boy. Anthony raised his forearm, blocking the blow—and was not prepared for the sheer force of it or the weight behind it. Anthony's tumble quickly turned into a controlled roll, and soon he was on his feet again, driving a fist as hard as he could into the side of the lunging man's head. It was a blow that would have TKO'd anyone in the sparring ring, but the huge man only staggered and shook his head.

Anthony was certain he'd broken his right hand on the man's thick skull... if the stabbing pain in his knuckles was any indication. Yes, he healed fast, but not that fast. For now, his right hand was useless to him.

Holding it against his side, he sidestepped another lunging masked figure, knocking the swinging hand away with his one good hand. Anthony swung a wild reverse kick that mostly landed. Okay, landed a lot. He looked back and saw the man skidding on the pavement... on his face.

Another came at him, flashing something in his hand. Another silver arrow. Anthony ducked under the first swipe, and blocked the nearly instantaneous second swipe. Anthony dropped and swept his leg around, taking the man's feet out from under him.

He had just stood and was about to turn and face his remaining attackers when an explosion of light appeared in his head, and he found himself spinning and stumbling. The biggest of the men, who appeared to have been waiting for the perfect opening, had blindsided him with two heaving fists. Anthony saw him coming again out of the corner of his eye, an eye that was awash in blood. Anthony, holding his damaged face, kicked out as hard as he could, and caught the advancing man in the gut, who stumbled back. Anthony couldn't clear his head. Never had he been hit so hard before. More blood spilled, he felt dizzy and sick. Just as he turned to face a man coming from his right side, someone from behind him plunged something deep into his shoulder.

Chapter 15

I heard, as if from a very, very far distance away, the words: "C'mon, Sam. Wake up."

Variations of said words continued to reach me from out of the darkness. Now, the words were followed by shaking—and the emptiness I knew coalesced into a focused consciousness, and soon, that same consciousness focused again within my 5'3" body that was presently lying back in the minivan's front seat.

"There you are! Geez, took long enough!"

It took me a full thirty seconds to remember where I was, and why I was waking up next to Allison in my van. She tried to help, no doubt seeing the confusion on my face, but her words, spoken too fast for my sluggish brain, did little to help.

And then, it all came rushing back to me. I was

here for a purpose, and that purpose was to get an audience with none other than Dracula himself.

"Shush," I said to Allison, reaching a finger out and pushing it against her flapping lips. "Please. Give me a minute."

"Fine way to treat your friend who just sat—"

"Allison..."

"Okay, fine."

She harrumphed and sat next to me, folding her arms under her chest. Her seatbelt was still on, I noted. Her phone was in her lap. I was willing to bet she had spent the entire time texting her friends and clients.

I sat up and rubbed my eyes and willed my brain and body back into service. Although I was out for only thirty minutes, it might as well have been an eternity.

I had died, I thought again, perhaps for the thousandth time in my life. *I had died and there was nothing out there for me. Nothing at all.*

As Allison took my hand to comfort me, I sought out Elizabeth. She had been given an assignment from me, and hopefully, from her own sojourn, would yield the help I needed. She had been eager to help. No surprise there.

Now, as I waited in the minivan with Allison, a mental image took shape in my mind. An image of a structure I knew all too well. A castle, in fact.

I turned to Allison just as she was turning to me —no doubt, she had seen the same structure in my thoughts. "I gotta go," I said.

"Wait! What about me? The van?"

"Stay here," I said.

"And wait again?"

I smiled at her. "Thank you for everything, sweetie. I appreciate it more than you know."

She smiled, too, but she didn't like being left behind.

I summoned the single flame, and saw within it a courtyard I was familiar with. A big open courtyard that I knew would be safe to leap to.

Now, I was moving toward the flame...

And then, I was gone.

Chapter 16

The courtyard wasn't quite as I remembered it.

What had once been a magnificent garden was now overrun with mean-looking weeds. If anything, the place looked abandoned. Even the pond had dried up. A pond where I had watched one of the Lichtenstein monsters walk right through, oblivious to the water. Indeed, Lichtenstein had created a wide range of monsters, many powerfully strong— stronger than even Kingsley, by a long shot. But many more were nothing more than walking husks. Those, I supposed, were his failures. He'd destroyed many of them with the strongest of his creations in a bizarre gladiator underground arena, where Lichtenstein himself had watched from high above.

That Dracula had moved in here was a surprise to me, but maybe it shouldn't have been.

Now, I turned my head away from the glare of

the hot sun and strode toward the cool shade of the covered hallways, then through the many archways and finally into what I knew was the main room. Oddly enough, I knew the interior of the castle intimately, having spent considerable time here while looking for a missing boy.

There was a fireplace here. And two camelback couches. Glass tables everywhere. A thick, polar bear rug sported an actual polar bear head. I suspected it was real as hell. That I was fascinated and not appalled by it suggested that Elizabeth was hovering a little too close for my comfort. But I left her there, for now.

My phone buzzed in my front pocket. I ignored it for now. It seemed prudent to keep my wits about me in Dracula's castle, which just so happened to be Dr. Lichtenstein's ex-castle, too.

After all, sitting before me—one leg crossed over the other and casually drinking from a goblet filled with a crimson fluid so deep that it appeared almost black—was the man himself, the ex-prince of Wallachia, one of the most feared men in history, impaler extraordinaire, and present receptacle of, perhaps, the most powerful dark master of them all. Or not. From what I understood, it was a toss-up between him and Elizabeth. Two very powerful entities who also happened to be in love—and who also desperately wanted to be together again. The problem being, of course, that one entity was in Dracula, and the other was in me. And for them to be together again... well, that just wasn't gonna happen. Not while I had any control of my body.

"Samantha Moon," he said genially, "to what do I owe this pleasure?"

Dracula, admittedly, looked like hell. No surprise there. He'd been roused from a deep sleep only minutes earlier. How Elizabeth had managed to do so, while Dracula had been in his own catatonic state, I didn't know. Perhaps Dracula, over time, had mastered awakening when need be. Perhaps he had an agreement with the entity within him to do, an entity named Cornelius.

"I seek help... Your Highness," I said, and for the life of me, I did not expect to hear those words come out of my mouth. Like, ever.

"So formal," he said, raising an eyebrow and standing effortlessly as I approached. He gestured to a chair across from him. Spanning us was a curved glass coffee table, upon which sat an array of dead flowers.

"I—I'm not sure why I said it, to be honest." Then it hit me: *Had it been her?* I didn't know.

That Dracula had been a monster during his reign went without saying. He'd killed and tortured and impaled and destroyed, and seemed to revel in it. At least, according to reports. I suspected he had made tough choices to control—that to rule with a heavy hand, and fear, was the order of the day. He had been a ruler, and a part of me—with a strong dose of Elizabeth thrown in for good measure—felt like he deserved the respect of his one-time office.

The dark prince snapped his fingers and a

female with a shining blue aura scuttled into the room, head bowed. She was topless, and wore only a short skirt. I noted the recent bite marks along her neck and back. Unlike the movies, these bite marks were more like bite *tears*. I suspected she had been bitten as recently as last night. No, not been... chewed upon, her skin broken open.

"Another glass, and put on a shirt. We have a guest."

I sensed the haughtiness in his voice. The strength. The exhaustion, too. He wasn't fully awake, but he was getting there. Mostly, I sensed his contempt for the woman. A very odd thrill surged through me.

No. Surged through *her... Elizabeth*.

Jesus, she was one whacked-out bitch.

As the semi-naked woman reached the room's threshold, it took all my willpower to say, "None for me, thanks."

Dracula's head snapped around to me. He looked genuinely perplexed. "Are you sure, Samantha? You look famished."

His words weren't a putdown, nor were they taken as one. Famished in my case meant I looked gaunt, thinner than usual. Perhaps I sported dark circles around my eyes, which, apparently, I sometimes did, according to Allison. Perhaps my hair hung languidly. Perhaps there was a noticeable lack of pep in my step. It was afternoon, after all. Hardly my brightest hour. I also suspected the prince had wanted to ply me with blood—human blood—which had proven to give Elizabeth more strength that I could readily handle. Enough strength, in fact, to potentially take me over completely. That would have suited Dracula just fine; in particular, it would have suited the entity within him, the entity who wanted Elizabeth, in every sense of the word.

I shook my head. "I'm fine." And to change the crap out of the subject, I said, "Tell me, how did you end up here?"

"In the monster's castle?"

"Yes."

He nodded, set his own goblet down. He sat back and folded his hands over one knee. "We take care of our own, Sam. Even when our own have done some very naughty things."

"What does that mean?"

"It means this castle needed a lot of cleaning, purifying perhaps. Although Lichtenstein was a creepy bastard, I couldn't let his castle fall into unsuspecting hands. There is still too much evidence here. We are still finding buried bodies."

That made some sense. He looked at me, waited. I swallowed, my throat suddenly dry. A drop of blood would have been nice. Damn nice. Finally, I said, "I need your help."

He looked at me some more, then waved off the woman who'd just returned to the room, now wearing a bloody shirt. Apparently, I didn't hide my disdain very well. Or at all.

"You don't approve, Samantha Moon?"

"Of course not. And you're going to release her, safe and sound."

"Am I now?"

"You will," I said.

"And what if I told you she was here of her own free will?"

"I would say you're full of shit."

I recalled my own inadvertent love slave. Russell Baker would have done anything for me. Anything. Even reduced himself to the role of household servant. But I hadn't let that happen.

"She satisfies my hunger, Samantha Moon."

"No, she satisfies the hunger of the bastard inside you," I said. "You could get along with animal blood."

"Could I now?"

I didn't answer. The bewildered amusement in his eyes was completely devoid of anger or resentment. If anything, he was completely enjoying this exchange. And, if I wasn't wrong—and I hoped like hell I was—he might have even been flirting with me. "Animal blood isn't the same, Sam."

"Trust me, I know."

"If I release her, then I will be without a source of replenishment."

"Then replenish your ass on a coyote or two."

Now, he threw his head back and laughed. "Sam, your naïveté is charming. Your code of honor is admirable. Your strength of will undeniable. Yes, I will release her, but he-that-is-within-me will demand another, and another. He needs to feed from the human source. Me, not so much. Quite frankly, I'm sick to death of blood."

Hearing Dracula himself tell me that he was sick to death of feeding on blood was so damn disarming that I took a moment to process the information. Finally, I said, "You would have killed her when you were done with her."

"Of course, Sam."

"You will release her, and you will do so tonight. And if you seek to be my friend, you will never kill again."

The cycle of killing had to end, and it had to end now, even if it meant waging an all-out war on Dracula.

I waited. Elizabeth stirred within me. I sensed her agitation. She didn't enjoy this sudden turn of events.

Dracula said, "Never is a long time for a vampire, Sam."

I continued waiting.

Finally, Dracula nodded and said, "For the sake of our budding friendship—and out of respect for an honorable woman who has proven herself to be, ah, rather dangerous—I will acquiesce to your wishes. For now, although I cannot promise forever."

I nodded. It was a decent compromise.

"Very well, then," he said, and summoned the woman again, who had already donned a dark blouse. After a minute or two of looking deep into her eyes—undoubtedly reaching deep into her psyche to find and release her true self—she stepped back and blinked. I suspected he'd also given her a handful of telepathic instructions, one being to not remember any of this. How long she'd been Dracula's love slave, I didn't know. Judging by the sheer amount of bite marks, I would say many months, maybe as long as Dracula had lived here in his new castle home.

I asked who she was and where she would go, and Dracula said she was a local prostitute, without family, friends, or home, surely not to be missed by anyone. Still, I didn't like the idea of sending her back out on the streets.

"She would be psychic by now," I said, thinking hard, "would she not?"

"Undoubtedly so," said Dracula, nodding. "Even if she'd only had a smattering of extrasensory talent, feeding from her would have increased it considerably..."

It would make her a powerful psychic, indeed. I said, "I'll be back for her as soon as I can. I know someone who can help her, someone who can put her to work."

"Very well, Sam. I won't feed from her again and... I'll release her to you when you return. After, I assume, you get what you came for."

"Information," I said. "And help."

As I spoke, my phone once again buzzed in my pocket. The third such call, but for the life of me, I couldn't imagine breaking away from this conversation, this bizarre scene—and not with this girl's very life hanging in the balance, and not in the presence of Dracula himself—to answer my cell phone.

At present, he was chuckling and shaking his small head. Dracula was, for all intents and purposes, a small man. Having originated from the fifteenth century, at an age when men rarely reached six feet tall, I suspected Dracula stood only a few inches taller than me. No doubt, he had been of average height for his time. He continued shaking his head, his eyes flashing fire. "There are not a lot of people who would come into my home —my new castle home, no less—and demand I release my food source, and then, in the very next breath, ask for my help."

"What can I say, I'm a maverick."

I also suspected Dracula *himself* liked me. That Dracula the man was interested in Samantha Moon the woman. I should not have been titillated by this, but I was, and I hated myself for it.

Poor Kingsley...

No, not poor Kingsley. I'd done nothing wrong. And there was nothing wrong with getting a kick out of receiving what might or might not have been flirtations of a past prince and warlord. It was exciting, and I wasn't going to feel bad for being excited.

But I did feel bad, a little. I loved Kingsley and I never wanted to betray him. Not even for the great Dracula's attentions and admiration.

Oh, well, I thought.

"I am being told through our mutual friends"—

he meant the dark entities within us—"that you seek answers about the original Dark Prince. Satan himself."

I nodded. "She told you about him?"

Dracula smiled from behind his goblet. His nose, I noted, was a little long and sharp for my taste. Okay, a lot long and sharp, but the strength he displayed in repose was palpable. I truly believed this man could move mountains. And armies, and change the course of history, vampire or not. "There are no secrets between us, Samantha Moon. Not when Elizabeth and Cornelius can meet in our mutual sleep."

"Meet where?"

"Another plane, Sam. Another world, perhaps. I am not privy to the machinations of the dark masters."

"Have you not asked?"

"I have."

"And?"

"And I was told to mind my own damn business, that I should be honored to be a receptacle for he who possesses me—that if not for him, I would have long since been dead, that he has given me eternal life, unheard-of gifts, and demanded very little of me, other than temporary use of my body when he sees fit."

"And am I speaking with him now?"

"No, Sam. He watches from the shadows."

"Tell me," I said after a moment. "What do you know of the devil?"

"A strange fellow, Satan," said Dracula, and I nearly laughed at the enormous understatement of his words, and the unlikelihood that I would have ever heard them in the first place. Dracula calling the devil a strange fellow.

Somehow, I kept my cool, and said, "Perhaps the strangest."

"Well put, Sam. Yes, he has waged a war, of sorts, against the dark masters, for they have slipped beyond his reach, which, from my understanding, frustrates him to no end."

"He says he's just fulfilling a role, a role created by mankind."

"Perhaps, Sam, but make no mistake, the devil delights in his work. His personal hells are a frightful thing to behold. Yes, I have spoken to him, Sam. A number of times, in fact. He has made offers to the entity within me, bargains, if you will. Bargains we have yet to take up. But I see you have made a deal with the devil. Tricky, that. And, really, his offer wasn't much, was it?"

"I could save two lives," I said.

"Yes, the lives of two humans. This is important to you, I see."

"Yes," I said, although sometimes, when Elizabeth was fighting for control of me, or too near the surface as she was now, it didn't seem so important. It seemed trivial. Humans seemed trivial. Like this little whore sitting across from us now...

I swallowed, closed my eyes, and demanded that Elizabeth step back—or she would be locked up again, for a very long time. I sensed her slinking back, retreating begrudgingly.

Dracula watched me curiously. At present, sitting here now in his living room, he did not have access to my current internal struggle with Elizabeth. Undoubtedly when I slept tomorrow morning, Elizabeth and Cornelius would have a meeting of the minds, so to speak, in their netherworld outside time and space, and she would fill him in on just how much she had gotten to me. But for now, my secret hunger and weakness were known only by me... and Elizabeth.

"Sam, would you like a snack? Something small?"

I blinked, coming back to my senses. "Snack?"

He raised his fingers to snap at the woman, thought better of it, gave me a lopsided grin, and stood. He left the room, then returned a minute later with a bowl full of... something.

I leaned forward as he set it on the coffee table between us. It was filled with... I didn't know just what. But one thing I did know, the inside of the bowl was moving, churning, roiling with spiny legs and wings.

I felt suddenly sick—but also oddly fascinated. "Mosquitoes?"

"But of course! They are such a delight." He looked at my confused and, undoubtedly, repulsed expression. "Surely you've had them before?"

"Er, no."

He roared with laughter and dipped his

fingertips inside the bowl... and extracted a handful of the critters. Then, with reckless abandon, tossed them in his mouth, one after another, as if they were living, squirming popcorn. As he chewed gleefully, he said, "Then let me fill you in on a secret, Sam. Mosquitoes make for very lively and delicious snack."

"Mosquitoes full of blood?" I said.

"But of course. We have no use for the unfed kind! Think of them as a sort of variety pack." He grinned and tossed another one in, chewed, grinned, spit out the remains in another, separate bowl. "Horse blood. Strong, sharp." He tossed in another. "Bovine, smooth, rich." He tossed in another and another. "Deer, rabbit. Ah, human! I just love when I get the human ones! They say they're good luck, you know."

I nearly asked who "they" were, but decided I probably already knew: vampires, of course. Instead, I said, "How... how did you manage to get a bowlful of recently-fed mosquitoes?"

Dracula, with bits of mosquito stuck between his teeth, grinned. He spit the latest tiny body into the bowl and said, "It's a handy skill to have, Sam, calling upon the animals of this world."

"Calling upon?"

"Yes, of course. Our telepathic communication extends far beyond humans; don't you know?"

"No, I didn't know."

"Do you not call upon your dragon in another realm, another dimension, another world, no less?"

"Well, yes..."

"Do you think your dragon friend speaks English?"

"Um..." I recalled Talos once stating that he found the correct words in my own thoughts, and used them. How he found them, and how he understood what they meant, I didn't know.

"Do you think I speak English to my own dragon? The answer is no. I speak medieval Romanian, my most comfortable of all tongues. The language of my ancestors, and the language of my internal dialogue. It is because telepathic communication is about energy and vibration and intent. It is the same for the creatures of our world, too."

"You communicate with the mosquitoes?" I asked, and tried like crazy not to laugh. Or, worse, snort.

"Remember that part about intent, Sam? With enough intention and focus, your call will be heard."

I must have had a look on my face. Perhaps it was my pre-snort look because he stood and strode over to the nearest window and pushed it open. Hot air wafted in. He came back, sat across from me, closed his eyes. A moment later, I heard the hypersonic buzzing.

A swarm of tiny dark shapes poured through the open window and into the sitting room. They swirled above the glass coffee table, forming a sort of black vortex. Had this been night, I would have seen their tiny, glowing bodies, too, as even the smallest of creatures sparked with a life force.

Dracula raised a hand and gestured, a number of the creatures peeled away from the vortex and filled the bowl before us, pouring in as if from a container in the sky. When the bowl was near to overflowing, Dracula swiped his palm, and the remaining mosquitoes circled once more, dispersed, and headed back through the open window.

Dracula reached over and fished out a plump one. "A freshly fed mosquito, as commanded by me. Here, try it. Hold out your hand."

Truth was, I could smell the fresh blood, coursing through all those tiny little spindly bodies. Sure, I might have missed the scent from one or two of them, but a bowlful of them was a different story. A bowlful might as well have been a bowl filled with fresh blood.

And the smell of it was driving me crazy. I held out my hand and Dracula dropped a fluttering creature into my palm. Although it seemed perfectly fine, it did not fly away. Indeed, it seemed to be moving in circles on my hand, its wings flashing haphazardly.

"It does not fly away," I said, curious.

"No, Sam. Nor will it. It is, quite frankly, waiting to be consumed."

I glanced at the woman sitting quietly in the chair, near the main archway into the room. Had she, too, been waiting to be consumed? Perhaps a part of her had been. But a deeper part of her had been trapped under the layers of suggestions, no doubt screaming to be heard.

We are monsters, I thought. *And the more I see, the more monstrous we are.*

The mosquito was fat from having recently fed. On what I didn't know, but the longer I held it the more I knew I couldn't resist. And, like eating a Tic-Tac, I popped it in my mouth.

I wanted to squirm. I wanted to laugh and say all the things anyone in their right mind would say in protest. But I didn't protest. Instead, I bit down and felt the small body pop sweetly over my tongue. I was instantly overwhelmed by one simple fact. It was completely delicious.

"Unlike me, Sam, you can consume its body."

Indeed, he had to spit the mosquito bits out, lest he risk vomiting them up later. I knew the feeling. My opal ring gave me the ability to eat anything, including mosquito bits, which I did now, swallowing.

"Pig blood," I said, nodding. "I know the taste well."

But this was different. This was fresh and warm and yummy.

"I imagine you do. Teach yourself to summon the animals of the earth, Sam. They will gladly feed you. Now, won't you have some more?"

I looked at his proffered hand, at the fluttering black bodies, then shook my head. Dracula shrugged and dropped them back into the bowl. I just couldn't risk inadvertently consuming even a droplet of human blood. At least, not right now, and not with Elizabeth so close to the surface.

My phone vibrated again. I nearly reached for it, but resisted. Something was going on, obviously. I sensed it now, but I was so close to getting my answers with Dracula, that I did something I rarely did. I reached into my pocket and, without looking at my phone, silenced it, even from vibrating.

I got right to it. "Help me find Danny," I said.

Dracula looked at me long and hard, his eyes flashing fire in the gloomy room. I sensed he was contemplating a bargain of his own; instead, I was pleasantly surprised when he said, "I cannot tell you where Daniel Moon is, for I do not know. But I can tell you where he isn't."

I waited, wondering where this was going.

Dracula sat back and crossed one leg over the other and adjusted the drape of his black jeans. "But to answer your question, Sam, I will need Cornelius to take over from here."

I inhaled, nodded. "Okay."

Dracula closed his eyes and dropped his head. A moment later, he shuddered. A moment after that, he raised his head and looked at me.

"Good afternoon, Sssamantha Moon."

Chapter 17

"You are Cornelius," I said.

"But of course."

Dracula the man sat across from me, hands in his lap, eyes slightly rolled up into his head, a grin forming on his face. Just a small grin, not quite the uncontrollable expressions I had seen from the biker, Taggart, a few days ago. One thing was obvious: Dracula had been taken over. Possessed thoroughly and completely.

He allowed it, I thought, mystified at such an agreement. *But I won't allow it. Not now, not ever...*

Elizabeth veritably exploded out of my mind upon hearing Cornelius' evenly-paced voice. But I stopped her cold. Commanded her to retreat, willing her to return to the shadows. I could have locked her up tight, but I didn't. I was, if anything, grateful to Elizabeth for arranging this little afternoon meeting, so I let her hang around. I let her listen, but no more than that. I had the image of a small child peeking from around the hallway corner at the adults speaking in the living room. Except this was no child I was dealing with. Not by a long shot.

"Won't you let my Elizabeth out, Sssamantha Moon?"

"No," I said. "End of discussion."

"You seek my help, but you won't give anything in exchange?"

"Not with you, and not with Elizabeth."

Dracula's—or Cornelius'—smile rose a fraction of an inch. Despite the forced smile, I knew Cornelius was not happy. Now, he turned his head this way and that, and I sensed he was getting comfortable in Dracula's skin. I also felt his eyes searching me, crawling over me.

"You are a pesky little bitch," he finally said.

"And you're a creepy asshole," I said. "And with that out of the way, let's talk."

His eyes rolled in the sockets. The half-smile on Dracula's face began a very slow retreat. "Very well, Sssamantha Moon. I will play by your rules, for now. It is enough to know that my Elizabeth is so very close. So very, very close."

He nearly reached out to touch me, and I nearly punched him in the face. Yes, Dracula I found interesting. This demonic, possessing, dark master inside him, not so much. That his female counterpart was within me was depressing to say the least.

He folded his hands in his lap, nodded, and seemed to regain control of himself—or over Dracula. He said, "The devil is no fool, Sam."

"Never said he was."

"There are no deals with the devil."

"I never made one. Not really."

"You are in agreement with him, Sssamantha. You are an agent for him, in effect. This is not good. You must move forward with caution."

"Duly noted."

"The devil is not a friend of ours, and, thus, no friend of yours. Remember that well."

"Not a friend. Got it."

"We have spent lifetimes seeking one like you, Sssamantha. You are invaluable to our plans. The devil knows this. He also knows that he cannot reach us."

"He seeks to destroy you, too."

"Of course, Sssamantha. We are beyond his reach. At least some of us are."

I knew who he was talking about. "Danny."

"A promising young recruit, your Daniel Moon..."

He wasn't mine. Not for a very long time, but I let it slide.

"...yesss, very promising. Unfortunately, he sided with an offshoot branch of our order."

"Offshoot?" I said. "Order?"

"Why, yes, Sam. An offshoot that conspired to kill you. Surely you do not think we want you dead, do you?"

"I'm leaning toward no?"

"We need you cooperative, if anything. Your bloodline and soul line are rare, Sam Moon."

"Soul line?"

"Your soul's evolution throughout the ages. You have steadily increased in strength. Indeed, in this lifetime, you would have been quite formidable."

"As a witch," I said.

"Indeed. But we had other plans for you."

I waited, and for a brief second or two, Cornelius blinked, and the cold eyes softened. I was certain that I saw the man who was Dracula watching me. But then, the eyes blinked again and Cornelius was back, his stare frosty and unblinking.

He said, "As you know, we seek she who can lift the veil. She who can pull back that which separates worlds. That which keeps us prisoners. You are she. You are that rare convergence of power."

I rolled my eyes. I could almost hear Tammy laughing at this. My sister, too. Then again, my sister had been kidnapped by the "offshoot" branch of which he had spoken. My sister, these days, found all of this terrible indeed. Still, the old Mary Lou would have laughed at the heavy melodrama of it all.

"Yay, me," I said.

"I do not understand—"

I cut him off. "Keep you prisoners *where*?" I asked.

"It is not wise to speak of this place to you, Sssamantha."

"Why?"

"Because you are not one of us. Not yet."

"Not ever. What is this business about an offshoot?"

He nodded. "A rival band of dark masters, Sssamantha. Although I am hesitant to call them dark masters. True, many have mastered the finer, darker arts, but many still are weak and some have not mastered even death, not completely."

"And they are your rivals."

"All are our rivals, Sssamantha." He paused. "Tell me, sssister... what is it that you fear so? Have we not given you eternal life? Eternal power? Have we not made you a god among man? Have you not seen many wonders? Is there not any gratitude inside you at all?"

I opened my mouth, ready for a quick retort, but then closed it again. Cornelius had, of course, hit upon one of my great internal struggles. Vampirism was both a blessing and a curse, in every sense of the words. Yes, I had been blessed with great powers, mind-blowing abilities, gifts of the rarest kind. But I had not asked for them. But I had been cursed, too. If the empty void was what awaited me in the afterlife—that is, if and when a silver dagger pierced my heart—then I had, indeed, been cursed to high heaven. Or *from* heaven.

And no. I wasn't about to thank the entities that were conspiring to fully take me over—and usher into this world the very plague that was them.

And so, I suggested—very politely and calmly —that he go fuck himself with something pointy and rough, something akin to what Dracula himself might have used to impale his many victims. Neither Dracula nor Cornelius seemed to like the suggestion, nor did they seem pleased with an angry and bitter Samantha Moon. An angry and bitter Samantha Moon wasn't pleased with them either. After all, they had caused much death, mayhem, and unrest. Especially in my own life.

Finally, Cornelius said, "You will see the light someday, Sssamantha Moon. You will see the light and you will come around to our side. Of this, I have no doubt."

"You should have doubts," I said.

"I will not try to convince you that you are better off now than you were before. That you have been given every gift known to man—"

"Except the gift of sunlight, food, and the afterlife."

"Food and sunlight are overrated. And immortality is yours."

"Until someone drives a silver dagger into my heart."

Cornelius smiled. It was, I noted, clearly not Dracula's slightly warmer smile. He said, "There are ways to avoid even that, Sam. Join us, and I will show you."

"Refer to the part where I said, 'go fuck yourself' and all that business with the stake and such."

Cornelius smiled and tilted his head. "Perhaps we should move on."

"A good idea," I said.

"Very well. Your Daniel Moon was not taught enough to cross into our world—our plane of existence, that is. But he was taught enough to avoid the dark one."

"The devil," I said.

"Yesss."

"And you know this how—wait, you have your spies."

"Of course, Sam Moon. We have eyes and ears everywhere."

"Creepy, but good to know. Tell me where I can find him."

"You are an investigator, are you not?"

"I am," I said. "And you're my best lead."

"Then let me give you a clue, Sssamantha Moon. He who is not proficient in the dark arts will gravitate to what is known."

"What does that mean?"

"I am but a humble dark master," said Cornelius.

"Bullshit. What do you know?"

"I know that not very long ago, a little boy let loose a low-level dark master. A dark master that had been bound to a book, no less—thanks, in part, to the work of a man you know well."

"Maximus," I said.

Cornelius winced, which didn't surprise me.

Archibald Maximus—and other alchemists like him, Light Warriors all—had, in fact, banished the dark masters to their present netherworld. An existence, I suspected, that was far from desirable, considering how much the masters sought to return.

"Yesss... *him*."

But I wasn't listening or thinking straight. My heart, normally dormant, had awakened with a fury, pounding in my chest, perhaps to alert me. It had to —since my own warning system had remained oddly silent, a warning system I was coming to realize that was meant only for me.

Not for my family.

And not for my son.

My son! I snatched my cell phone from my pocket, and saw that I had missed twenty-two phone calls, and countless text messages. The one on top was, perhaps, the scariest message I have ever received. Ever.

"Mom!!" Tammy had texted. "They took Anthony! Where R U???"

Chapter 18

I reappeared in my minivan, praying like hell there wasn't anything or anyone sitting in the front seat. Like Allison's purse. Or Allison's booty, for that matter. She knew enough about what I did and how it theoretically worked to leave a space for me to return. I hoped.

My seat, mercifully, was empty.

Allison, who sat hunched over her phone in the passenger seat, promptly screamed when I reappeared. She dropped her phone, and by the time she had picked it up again from the floor mat, I was mostly through the worst of the disorienting dizzy spell.

"Sam! Oh my God, Sam. Everyone's been trying to reach you—"

"Just tell me what happened." I had reached for my own phone but didn't want to waste the time scrolling through the messages. "What happened to Anthony?"

She shook her head—and tears sprang from her eyes. "I didn't know what to do, Sam—if I left and you never got the message—or moved the van somewhere you weren't expecting it to be—or—"

"Never mind all that, goddammit! What happened to Anthony?"

"They got him, Sam—"

"Who?"

"I don't know."

"Where?" I was already starting the minivan.

"His school—"

I could teleport, but I didn't know where, exactly. A part of me didn't care who saw me appear out of thin air. But I couldn't take the chance of teleporting into someone or something. Besides, his school wasn't very far at all.

Gunning the minivan, I whipped through the alley behind Alicia's—and exploded out onto Berry Street. Once there, I floored it, caring little for the safety of others or for the law—and trusting my instincts and cat-like reflexes to keep us alive long enough to reach Anthony's school.

***

There were a half dozen of us in the principal's office, including Detective Sherbet and a recently-arrived Kingsley Fulcrum. Not able to reach me, in desperation, Tammy had called Kingsley. Allison sat with Tammy just outside the closed door.

I knew Tammy was scanning anyone and everyone's mind for any possible lead. She'd told me this between her hysterical apologies and before Allison could take her hand and sit with her, echoing my own words that none of this was her fault.

Whatever *this* was.

A kidnapping, I thought. *In broad daylight.*

My son...

The spacious office was buzzing. Officers and detectives spoke urgently. Phones rang. Walkie-talkies crackled. Someone shouted. Sherbet was huddled with the principal as I paced in a fast, tight circle, running my fingers through my hair, wanting to pull my hair out, too. Wanting to hurt everyone in the room.

My mind wasn't right, wasn't here either. It certainly wasn't making heads or tails of the myriad of voices and phone calls and shouts I was hearing. I already knew there was a camera crew positioned in front of the school. I had no idea how many cruisers were flashing out front. Ten? Twenty? Maybe more. People everywhere. Voices everywhere. Some crying. Loud, hysterical gasps coming from me, gasps I couldn't control.

More pacing. Pushing fingers through my hair. Sherbet speaking to me. No idea what he said. Buzzing everywhere. Static in my ears.

I shouldn't be here. I should be finding my boy, hunting down the fuckers who took him.

Who took him?
Who took him?

No one knew. I heard the words, "masked assailants" and "black van." I heard the words "abduction." I heard the words, "He put up a hell of a fight." I heard the words, "never seen anything like this before." I heard the words, "all hands on deck," and "intensive search." I knew there was an APB on the van, along with an Amber Alert. I knew that everyone and anyone was looking for my son. Except he hadn't turned up, not yet.

I also heard something else, something else that was repeated often: "Second abduction in three years."

I had known about the first abduction, of course. I knew a girl had been abducted walking home from Anthony's middle school three years ago. She'd never been found, nor had her abductors. There had been no real tips, either, and certainly no arrests.

I heard more words, too, incomprehensible words, words that seemed to come from everywhere at once. Promises that we would get him back. Most sounded sincere. Most didn't know how to sound.

Mostly, no one knew anything.

Nothing. Nothing at all.

I paced.

I'm always the cool one, I thought. *I'm always the collected one. The one who thinks clearly.*

But I couldn't. Not now. Maybe not ever again. My mind was spinning, spinning. Out of control...

Lord, please help him, I managed to pray. *Please help my baby boy.*

Two support technicians were poring over the school's security set-up, bringing up files, bringing up video. Most police forces hired such civilian technicians, along with many other non-investigative jobs. The techs were good. I knew them by name. Had worked with them on a number of other cases. I knew one of them knew the security camera system well. Now, he had isolated the footage.

Sherbet watched it, glancing at me once or twice. Now, he wanted me with him, to watch it, too. But I shook my head. I couldn't watch it. Not now, not now. No, no—just no, goddammit!

But he wouldn't have it. He needed me. Needed my input. Time was of the essence.

My baby boy...

He took my elbow, yanked me around. It was harsh, rough, but I wouldn't have responded otherwise. I blinked at him through tears.

"We need you to see this, Sam."

"Detective... help me..."

The alarmed look on his face softened with a slow blink. Beyond him, I could see Kingsley studying the principal's computer screen. The men were riveted, shaking their heads, and then, wincing... and finally dropping their heads.

"You need to see this, Sam."

I nodded. Yes, of course. I understood. But then, I shook my head and burst into tears, and the detective pulled me in close—and when I'd had a good cry, I was startled to find myself in Kingsley's arms. At some point, Kingsley and the detective had traded places. At least, that's what I hoped. Either that, or I had completely lost my marbles.

"Sam," said Kingsley, looking down at me, his shaggy hair hanging forward. "We need you. Your son needs you."

"I know," I said, nodding, but the tears came again and again.

"Sam," he whispered, shaking me a little. And a little for Kingsley was actually a lot. I think I might have looked like a bobble-head toy. Little did the others know that Kingsley couldn't hurt me. Not really. And he needed to be rough with me. He needed to shake me out of it.

Finally, I took in some air, and he shook me again, but this time, I knocked his hands away went into his arms... into the comforting solidness that I knew and loved. That was what I needed from him. A huge bear hug that gave me strength. He said very softly in my ear, "I'm here for you, Sam. No matter what it takes, we'll find him."

Sherbet made room for me on the other side of the desk. And with Kingsley and Sherbet on either side, the detective reached out and pressed "Play" on the oversized touch-screen monitor.

Within seconds, I saw my son standing alone in front of the school. I watched him kick something too small to see—a rock maybe—but Anthony seemed pleased with himself. I knew that look all too well.

It was then that the black van stopped in front of him.

And all hell broke loose.

Chapter 19

Worst. Three. Minutes. Ever.

Standing there and watching the men surround my son—and watching him fight for his life, was hell on earth for me. I took some consolation in watching him dispatch two of the larger men. Two of the very fast men. Lightning-fast. Except my son was just that much faster.

Not just any men, I thought.

The first time through, I was sick and sweating and holding myself, even as Kingsley held me. I screamed when the man rose behind my son, wielding the silver-tipped arrow like a dagger. My mouth dropped open and something pitiful and terrible and sorrowful came out of me when the arrow plunged down, down into my son's shoulder.

My son's shoulder.

His shoulder. A little boy's shoulder. A

shoulder I had held in my hands when he was so very tiny—

He threw back his arms and cried out, and it was then that the other men pounced... and dragged him into the open van. A moment later, a cell phone was tossed out through the van doors. My son's cell. Then the doors slammed closed and the van squealed off. It had happened so quickly. No one had time to react, and, in the video, the poor old lady who did come to his aid was still lying face-first on the pavement. I would thank her later. I would check on her later...

Later...

The license plate turned out to be a fake. That plate number had never been issued.

I had the techs replay the stabbing over and over. I had to verify my son was alive. I had to know the arrow had not found his heart, even if through the shoulder.

I saw my son look up as they dragged him to the van, saw him look at one of the men who was waiting just inside the van. Their eyes lingered. I was sure of it. My son was okay. Why had their eyes lingered?

Knowing my son had made it out of here alive gave me hope. And with hope came rage. I let it grip me, take hold of me, because rage felt better than losing hope. With the rage, I saw answers. With the rage, I saw myself killing each of the men, slowly, quickly, painfully. There was a lot of blood in this mental image. Blood and lost limbs.

I had quit crying, too. The tears had stopped the instant the van had appeared. The tears were replaced first by horror and sickness, and then red-hot fury. Now, even the fury was gone. Fury wouldn't find my son. Cool heads would. My cool head.

I breathed, paced, breathed, talked myself down.

I would kill them all.

Every last piece of shit.

His shoulder. His poor, sweet shoulder.

The fuckers.

I was back behind the monitor, nodding, and the tech played it through again, and again. We were all looking for something telling. Anything. After the van sped off, other people had appeared in the security footage, teachers and students, some of whom chased after the van.

We went through it again and again. I forced myself to watch, and to see beyond my son fighting for his life. To look for answers. I forced myself to watch the man take aim with the crossbow, watched my son's impressive reflexes and fighting skills, watched him dispatch man after man, not realizing —or perhaps realizing, but fighting on anyway because that was all he could do—that the men were not like other men. Normal men would have stayed down. Normal men weren't this fucking big.

These were not normal men.

I paced again, but this time with hands clenched. I ran my fingers through my hair. Too roughly—my longish, pointed nails inadvertently slashed my scalp. I felt the blood appear. Someone handed me a tissue, I snatched it and blotted the blood, but could feel my skin already healing.

"Get them out," I said to Sherbet.

"Who—"

"Everyone! Get them all out! Kingsley, you stay. Detective, you stay, too."

Sherbet nodded, jerked his thumb toward the only door. A half-dozen other detectives raised their eyebrows and murmured to each other, but they got moving. The principal demanded to stay—that is, until he got a look at my face, my eyes, and I didn't need telepathic suggestion to get him moving, too.

The detective shut the door and came over to where I was now standing with Kingsley behind the desk, staring down at the frozen image of my son in the act of kicking a rock, just before all hell would break loose, just before he would be stabbed in the shoulder, and ripped from my life.

"Okay, Sam, the floor is yours."

I looked at Kingsley; Kingsley looked at me. I said, "These weren't men. Not mortal men, at least."

The detective looked even sicker, paler, sweatier. "Okay, give me the worst. What are we dealing with? Goblins? Trolls?"

I nearly laughed. Nearly. No, that wasn't true. I wasn't close to laughing at all. But a part of me—a very deep part of me, a part that had nothing to do with Elizabeth—appreciated his small attempt to add a touch of humor here, especially since he really didn't know what the hell he was talking about. The sad thing was, Anthony would have guffawed at the detective's supernatural naïveté. Once Anthony knew what naïveté meant, that is.

"Werewolves," said Kingsley.

Sherbet exhaled through tight, pursed lips, an exhale that warbled into a nasally whistle. He sounded like an old, tired teakettle.

The detective might have picked up on that mental image of mine, because he gave me a quick sidelong glance, then said, "Why would werewolves want your son, Sam?"

I knew why, of course. Just a few months ago, I was told that my family lineage went all the way back to her Hermes Trismegistus, the original alchemist. And those within his bloodline sported a rather beautiful and rare calling card: a silvery serpent that wound through our auras. Many in my lineage were recruited to join other alchemists, becoming what was called Light Warriors. Others were discovered by the baddies in the world—often destroyed at young ages, wiped off the planet before they could even be trained to become said warriors. And not just wiped off... but consumed. The Hermes bloodline, the blood itself, gave immortals an invaluable and highly desirable edge.

Rather than explain all this, I gave Sherbet access to my thoughts, and soon, he was nodding grimly. "I get it, Sam—but I also don't get it, too. You know?"

"I know," I said.

He turned to Kingsley. "Do you know them?"

"More than likely. There're not many of us, and noticeably fewer after Samantha and her old friend dispatched a pack of them a few years back."

I felt something inside me snap, something that had been waiting to snap. Something that helped me focus all my anger and rage. And that something was Kingsley.

"Wait a fucking second," I said, I grabbed his shoulder and spun him away from the monitor. No mean feat. "You *more than likely* know of a pack of kidnappers? Child killers? And all the while, you've let these fuckers walk the streets—"

"Hold on, Sam—"

I pounded his chest with a fist. If it hurt or fazed him, he didn't show it. "No, you wait, you son of a bitch. Letting these monsters roam the streets makes you complicit, and if anything happens to Anthony—anything at all—I will fucking hate you for the rest of my fucking life. And that's going to be a long-ass time—"

"Sam, please—"

But I couldn't stop. I saw only red fury and I wanted to hurt Kingsley, and I wanted to hurt those who hurt my son so much more. I wanted to rip them from limb to limb and burn each limb. And then, burn them some more.

"Jesus..." said Sherbet, picking up on thoughts that Kingsley couldn't hear or see.

"Sam," he said, "I have no way of controlling

these guys, nor could I have known they were capable... of such a thing. Just as you have no way of knowing the depth and depravity of the local vampires. No one could ever expect you to find them all and hunt them down."

I understood his logic. But I still hated him. Or wanted to hate him. Yes, how could he have known they were capable of... this?

Now, Kingsley took hold of my shoulders. "Believe me, Sam. Had I known any of them were capable of such a heinous, brazen, despicable act, they would have long since been dead."

I had another round or two of tears, and Sherbet gently cleared his throat, and when I turned and looked at him, I saw the many emotions crossing his reddish face. I also heard his thoughts. He didn't like any talk of killing, especially around him. He didn't understand what was happening, but he did understand that he was going to face a lot of people, including his own captain, who themselves were going to have to face the media about how and why a middle-school boy had been kidnapped at a public school in broad daylight.

Mostly—and I loved the detective for this with all my heart—he wanted to find my boy, and he wanted to find him now.

Enough with the tears, I told myself. *Enough with the blame. Enough with anything that has nothing to do with finding my son.*

The feed had been rewound again. On the screen, thanks to the wide-shot of the camera, I could see the black van approaching, east along Orangethorpe Avenue. The van had no plates, as had been noted earlier by Sherbet. The three of us gathered back around the monitor again, and Sherbet fast-forwarded to when the smallish, masked man came into view on the screen, the man sitting inside the van itself. He had not wanted to engage, clearly keeping back, and clearly fascinated.

"Here's the anomaly," said Sherbet. "Can either one of you tell me who he might be... as in what kind of creature."

"Unfortunately, I can't read auras through TV, or security footage," said Kingsley.

"Auras, the light around bodies," said Sherbet. "Or lack thereof."

"You're learning, Detective," I said. "Immortals have no auras."

"Your son's aura was black, at one point," Sherbet pointed out, recalling our conversation from years ago.

"Yes. A sign of imminent death," I said.

"So, you can't tell if the guy in the van is, say, a vampire or not?" For once, the grizzled detective didn't look sick to the stomach while asking such a ridiculous question.

"He's not a vampire," said Kingsley, moving up to the screen.

I nodded and pointed, my fingertip touching the crap out of the nice monitor. "His neck and arms are exposed. And no ring."

"And no obvious sunscreen," said Kingsley.

"Even with sunscreen, he would have been in a world of hurt," I said. "And he's not even trying to shy away from it."

"Unless he's wearing another medallion," said Kingsley.

"Maximus has destroyed the only known one, a medallion he created, mind you."

"Unless there's more than one and he's not telling you the truth," said Kingsley, glancing at me and looking away. Kingsley had dropped hints in the past that he wasn't entirely sure that Archibald Maximus could be trusted. I tended to disagree, and defended Maximus to no end, certain that Kingsley's concern arose from jealousy, and not anything tangible.

I waved off his asinine comment, and, with enough finality in my voice to permanently put an end to the subject, I said, "There are no more medallions."

"Enough about the damn medallions," said Sherbet, and he jabbed a flat, squarish fingertip at the screen. "Your son recognized one of them. Look."

He played it again and we looked: Anthony, just after avoiding the first arrow—and after leaping forward and taking out the shooter in what could only be described as an impressive feat of strength and agility—he paused and glanced into the back of the van, where the man was sitting. No, not just glanced. Paused and stared, even if for a fraction of a second. I had Sherbet fast-forward to where the gang of men dragged my son into the van, to where my son looked over at the man again, to where I was sure their eyes made contact.

"What do you think?" asked Sherbet, looking at us. "The two of you ruled out he was a vampire."

"A teacher?" asked Kingsley.

"One of his *own* teachers?" I added, and my own question just felt right to me. Damn right. *Sweet Jesus...*

Detective Sherbet said, "I'll get the principal."

Chapter 20

A short, agonizing while later, Mr. Russo, the middle-school principal, reported back to us. "All but two of his teachers are accounted for."

"And the other two?" I asked.

"Mrs. Little, his English teacher, has been home all week, sick. And Mr. Matthews, his algebra teacher, who isn't picking up." Russo paused, then added, "We compared Ericka Tanner's class schedule—"

"Who?" asked Kingsley.

"The student who disappeared after school three years ago," said Russo, looking pained all over again. Kingsley nodded and the principal went on: "She and Anthony shared a common teacher."

"Mr. Matthews," I said. It had, after all, been a smallish man on the surveillance video. Not a woman.

The principal nodded, and truly looked sick to his stomach.

"Describe Mr. Matthews," said Sherbet.

"What do you mean—"

"How tall?" I snapped. "Big guy, little guy? Fat, thin?"

"Medium, I would say. Medium all around."

I looked at Sherbet, then at Kingsley, and we all nodded. I took in a lot of air, and saw a lot of red, too.

Sherbet pulled out his department-issue cell and made a phone call. Shortly after that, he read off Matthews' cell number. We waited. I wanted to pull my hair out while I waited. I also wanted to hurt someone very badly. A lot of someones.

"Thank you," said Sherbet after a minute and disconnected the call. He turned to us. "I'm getting a court order to ping his cell phone."

"Ping?" asked Russo.

"Locate his phone," said Sherbet. "With luck, it could lead us right to him."

Or them, I thought. *To Anthony.*

"Meanwhile," said Sherbet, turning to the principal, "get me Matthews' home address. Now."

Chapter 21

Once in the van, the ropes had appeared instantly, looping around and around him.

The men had removed their hoods—and Anthony instantly recognized his math teacher, Mr. Matthews, sitting off to one side and watching him, swaying with the speeding van. A rag had been shoved into Anthony's mouth. Anthony was pretty sure he could spit out the rag, but he hadn't tried. No one seemed to care that a thirteen-year-old boy was sporting a silver-tipped arrow from his shoulder. The arrow had hurt at first, but mostly it had been a shock to his system. Now, he was only barely aware of it. If anything, it was a minor irritant, especially when the ropes pulled at it.

No one spoke in the van, and no one spoke when they transferred him into a car with tinted windows. The guy sitting next to Anthony in the backseat was sporting a round shiner under his eye. Anthony could barely believe the shiner was from him. Anthony wasn't scared, not really. Not yet, at least. He didn't know what was happening, but he didn't think these guys could really hurt him. Anthony knew he was acting a little cocky, but being cocky was all he had right now. He also knew that if they gave him even a sliver of a chance to escape, he would do so. No way these big guys were going to catch him. No freakin' way.

So, he sat, and waited, and ignored the irritant in his shoulder, and wondered where they were taking him, and wondered, too, where his mom was. Anthony almost—*almost*—felt sorry for these goons. His mother, though smaller, was going to tear their heads off. Kingsley, too.

Oh, yes. Especially Kingsley.

***

Anthony counted four of them.

Silver-tipped arrows, that is. Each had been plunged into various points of his body, each hurting worse than the one before it—at least initially. The pain mostly went away. Mostly. The arrow in his stomach hurt the worst of all, and *that* pain wasn't going away so quickly, probably because he could feel it grating against what he was sure was his spine.

Minutes earlier, two of the men had hauled Anthony from the old car, which had been parked inside what appeared to be a factory or a warehouse. Anthony wasn't sure what the difference was, but many of his video games were often set in places like this: massive buildings stacked with boxes and bins and metal shelves, with dusty rafters overhead that were perfect for lassos or whips or to run along.

A dusty overhead light revealed that he was in a room of sorts. Not a real room, because there were no actual walls, unless you counted the staked wooden crates and cardboard boxes that surrounded him. There had been a chair waiting for him under that dusty light bulb. Directly beneath the chair was a drain. The drain was rusted and the whole place smelled sort of like copper—and something else, something kind of rotten. He didn't know the smell. The way the weak light lit up the metal chair seemed ominous—except Anthony wasn't really sure if he was using that word right. *Ominous*. Yeah, it felt right, whatever it meant, although he was sure he had read it in books and had heard his mom use it.

They had shoved him down into the chair, and only then had Anthony realized the chair was much more than a chair. It had manacles along the armrests—and even manacles along the front legs. It took all the guys in the room—too many to count accurately, although there did seem to be more now —to hold him down while they removed the ropes and locked his arms and legs into place. Anthony hadn't seen any chance to escape during the process, which made him nervous. How many more chances would he have to escape? He didn't know.

Mostly, he watched them and tried to memorize their faces, their voices, anything that might help his mom find them later. His mom was really, really good at finding the bad guys. And these were very bad guys, indeed. Maybe the worst ever. Soon, they were satisfied that he wasn't going anywhere. Maybe he really wasn't.

Anthony was about to discover they weren't done with him yet.

Not by a long shot.

***

The arrow in his stomach hurt the most.

Every breath, every small movement, and it seemed to dig deeper, doing more and more damage. He quickly realized that crying made it worse. So, he stopped crying, and stopped moving, as much as possible. He noticed, with some alarm, that he didn't need to take as many breaths as he had thought. He could hold his breath, in fact, for far longer than he'd ever realized. And so, for long periods of time, he sat completely motionless, still in pain, but not as much.

He was alone for now, although he could hear voices coming from what he thought was another room nearby, voices he recognized as those of his captors.

Anthony was interested to discover a few things. One, he wasn't really that scared. Two, he knew, deep down that his mother would find him, no matter how much these guys hurt him or tried to scare him. And three, he knew he would escape.

He knew it, and believed it, with all of his heart. But most interesting to Anthony, as he sat in the quiet space under the single light bulb and surrounded by boxes and crates, was the soft whispering he heard in his head. A soft whispering that, oddly, sounded a bit like his dad. The words came to Anthony whole and complete, telling him everything was going to be okay.

Everything is going to be okay...

Obviously, the words weren't his actual father, but Anthony found them comforting. He liked them. He liked them a lot. He especially liked that they sounded like his father, who he missed so much. So much.

"Everything is going to be okay," Anthony whispered to himself, nodding. "And I'm going to escape... oh, yes..."

As he fought a wave of pain in his stomach, Anthony saw movement behind the boxes to his left. There was something in the air, something in the air maybe. Something swirling. Maybe a dust devil?

Except this something, this dust devil, was all black and it was not very far from where Anthony sat tied to the chair, and now, it was swirling faster and faster.

Anthony had thought he was brave. In fact, he'd been proud of himself so far. Heck, he wasn't afraid of these men. And if he could just get out of these ropes, he would show them what he could really do to them.

But as the swirling blackness took form before him, Anthony began to know real fear. More fear than he had ever known before.

Because directly before him, taking on more and more shape, expanding and growing and solidifying, and now growling deep within its massive chest—was the biggest dog Anthony had ever seen.

A dog with three heads.

Chapter 22

Outside the office, I pulled Allison and Tammy aside and gave them the news. Tammy held my hand with both of hers, crying harder than I had seen her cry in her life.

Her crying was contagious, and I fought the tears, and so did Allison.

"They really took him, Mom?" asked Tammy between the tears. "This is real?"

"It's real, baby."

"But who?"

"I don't know yet—"

"Yes, you do. Mr. Matt—"

"Shh! Not so loud. We don't know for sure."

"But you're going there now, to his house." Tammy paused, cocked her head, spotted Sherbet coming out of the office with his cell phone pressed in his ear. "Sherbet is calling a judge, a friend of his, asking for a search warrant."

"He is, now be quiet. We don't know for sure if Mr. You-Know-Who is involved. He might not be."

"But he might be. I want to go, Mom. I'll tell you if he's lying."

"I can do that on my own—"

"Unless he's a vampire or something else, then you can't. But I can."

"She has a point," said Allison.

I was about to tell my friend to stay out of it, and I was about to be nasty because I was still not myself—and I wouldn't be myself until I found Anthony—but I took a deep breath, looked at both of them, my powerful friend, and my powerful daughter. Truth was, I could use both of them.

"Exactly, Mom," said Tammy. "Anthony's going to need all the help he can get. The detective got the search warrant."

I blinked, amazed all over again by my daughter.

Not trusting myself to drive, I handed the keys to Allison, and soon, we were following Sherbet's unmarked vehicle through the tangle of cruisers and news vans.

Kingsley trailed us in his own black SUV.

***

I scanned the house, using a trick of my own, and verified the place was empty, except for a sleeping cat.

The door was locked, too; that is, until Kingsley put a shoulder into it. Then the whole thing went down in a heap, along with most of the doorframe. A cat scrambled over the linoleum, trying to find purchase, its face a rictus of unabashed fear. Finally, its paws found enough traction to rocket it down the hallway and out of sight. It would have been funny under just about any other circumstance. Or not. The little guy nearly had a heart attack.

Sherbet winced at the door falling in, but I mentally reassured him that by the time everything was said and done—and by the time we found my son safe and alive—no one would remember the destruction of property. I would make sure of it.

We spread out. I paused often and scanned, projecting my thoughts forward—this time into closets and showers and behind anything and everything. Yes, we were alone.

I checked my cell. 3:42 p.m. My son had been forcibly kidnapped at 2:38 p.m. Over an hour and counting. That Mr. Matthews wasn't here seemed to indict him even more. But we needed more than an indictment. We needed to know where the hell they took my son.

The house was smallish. From my scans, I already knew it was a two-bedroom, one-bathroom deal. It was also old. Of course, he was living on a teacher's salary. Principal Russo had confirmed Matthews was single and had been for as long as he'd known him.

On the drive over, I had confirmed there was no Facebook page or LinkedIn page for Matthews, no Twitter or Instagram. There had been, however, a picture of him on the school's website, which I had copied and text-messaged Sherbet, Allison and Kingsley. I'd asked Tammy, who had been sitting in the back of the minivan, if this was our guy, flashing his pic on my cell phone at her. She nodded, but reminded me that she'd never had one of his classes, although she was sure that was him. Tammy was a few years removed from middle school now.

Now in the home, I saw framed pictures of his cat, and that was it. No pictures of family or friends. Just framed cat pictures. Presumably, the same one who'd nearly split itself trying to run in two different directions to get away from us. Apparently, cats had an aversion to werewolves. Go figure.

The floors creaked as we fanned out, looking for anything that would suggest Matthews' part in the kidnapping of my son. Even better, where they might have taken my son. What that anything was, we didn't know. But each of us trusted our instincts. Kingsley focused on Matthews' bedroom. I found myself at his desk, which was located in one corner of the living room. Sherbet was poking through the kitchen, going through mail and piles of paper.

We all moved with purpose, speed. I forced myself to look as calmly as possible, not wanting to miss anything. Sometimes the smallest clue was the biggest break.

My baby, I kept thinking. *My baby.*

Even as I searched, even as I forced myself not to drop to my knees and just completely freak out, I kept the mantra going in my head:

My baby, my baby.

It was on repeat, and that was okay. I didn't need to think of anything else. I didn't *want* to think of anything else. So, as I searched, I let instinct take over.

I noted the empty desktop. I noted the dusty indication that a laptop had recently been removed from this space. My guess, he took his laptop to and from school. I glanced around; no laptop bag, either. Today, he'd never made it home. I bit my lip. Having his laptop would have been damn helpful.

"Having anything would be damn helpful," said Sherbet, tossing aside a handful of unopened letters that looked to be bills. "At least, that's what I think you said. Hard to make out your thoughts with all that 'my baby' going on."

"Sorry—"

"Don't be, Sam. We're all freaking out here. "

Kingsley came back, shaking his shaggy head, and barely fitting through the narrow hallway. The house shook with each of his steps. As he approached, I suddenly knew what I was looking for. Knew it without a doubt. Whether it was here or not, I didn't know, but I was suddenly a woman with a plan.

I nearly bowled over Sherbet as I moved

through the small and dusty living room. I felt both sets of men's eyes on me, and sensed Sherbet's concern for me. He and he alone had access to my thoughts, which I didn't bother shielding. There was nothing to shield anyway. He heard the running patter of my thoughts, and saw me suddenly scouring the living room, and could only wonder if I was losing it.

The living room wasn't very big—and I'm sure I looked like a crazy woman as I tossed aside magazines, and scanned all the outlets, looking for telltale signs. Nothing in the living room or kitchen. I headed into the bathroom—and there, under a pile of science fiction novels stacked on the toilet tank was something I had sensed was here, but couldn't have possibly known. And deep down, I could only wonder if my own psychic senses were developing. They had to be. Hell, maybe they were developing out of necessity. As in, the necessity of finding my son.

Either way, I tossed aside the Asimov and Howey novels and saw my prize: A Samsung Galaxy mini-tablet computer.

***

It still had some power, too.

We were in the kitchen, with both men crowded behind me as I powered it on, praying like crazy that the tablet wasn't password protected.

The Samsung logo appeared on the screen,

unspooling like magic. I knew that most tablets weren't as locked down as phones or even computers. Mostly forgotten, tablet computers were a gateway to personal information. The screen cycled through... and I breathed a sigh of relief when the home screen opened before us.

"Good thinking," said Kingsley. He was leaning next to me, and I couldn't help but notice the longish hair that had recently sprouted from between his knuckles. Yes, between. As in, within the last hour; indeed, with tonight's full moon and sunset just hours away, Kingsley was already beginning his own transformation.

"You'll be turning soon," I said.

"I can fight it. For a little while."

I doubted he could, but I didn't say anything. I had seen him in the process of turning last year, and it had been... rigorous, to say the least. The monster within him was not to be denied. But I appreciated his support. The problem being: if we were facing down a pack of werewolves—and judging by the size and speed of the men, it seemed obvious that we were—then my boyfriend himself was susceptible to the same changes they were going through. Which meant, my boyfriend would be of no help at all, and I knew this was killing Kingsley. I patted his shoulder, and nearly recoiled. The sheer amount of heat coming off him was staggering.

Sherbet was on the phone, talking urgently, barking orders. He clicked off and reported, "We located Matthews' cell and car."

I looked up, my mouth opening.

Sherbet quickly shook his head. "The car was parked at a Taco Bell a few miles away, the cell in the trunk. No sign of Matthews anywhere. We're contacting Taco Bell to release their own surveillance footage. My bet, we'll catch him parking the car... and then walking away, but you never know."

I nodded, willed myself to stay strong, calm. Finding his cell—and Matthews—would have been ideal. I said, "It was a long shot, but worth taking since the van's plate turned out to be a fake."

He nodded. "We could have lucked out, Sam. Your son, Matthews, and his cell could have been all in one place."

"Meanwhile," I said, holding up the tablet computer, "we have this."

Chapter 23

I'm dreaming, thought Anthony.

He'd heard his mother say those very same words often enough, usually under her breath, and usually alone. Sometimes, he would hear her in her office or alone in the living room or even the kitchen. His hearing was that good. Often, she would whisper the words in the bathroom, of all places, but he knew why: Mommy couldn't see herself in the mirror, and he knew it totally freaked her out.

Now, he heard himself saying them, too, over and over, sounding just like his mother. And if he wasn't saying them, he was sure thinking them, because never in all his thirteen long years could he have imagined seeing what he was seeing now.

But there it was, bigger than any dog he had ever seen, and not just because of its three heads. It was easily as big as a horse, maybe even bigger than a moose, if moose were bigger. Anthony wasn't sure. Anyway, its chest was packed with muscle. In fact, the whole dang thing looked like one big pile of walking, bulging muscle. And it was black, so black that it looked like a moving shadow. But Anthony saw the teeth, saw the dripping drool, and, most of all, saw the flickering eyes.

Like everyone else, Anthony had heard the reports of the three-headed dog. It had been the talk of school today. Word had it that a whole street of people had reported seeing it. People were saying it was an optical illusion. A hologram. A video game company pulling a stunt, maybe.

It had sounded so awesome. Anthony had wished like crazy he'd been one of those lucky enough to see it, even if it had been a Hollywood stunt or something. The police had been concerned enough to ask his mother to look into the reports, according to Tammy. But that's all his sister would say on the subject. At the time, Tammy had seemed scared. She had seen something she wasn't telling him, something inside their mom's mind. Sometimes, Anthony was glad he couldn't read minds.

Now, of course, Anthony knew it hadn't been a trick or a hologram. The thing coming toward him was massive and real, and it was kicking up dust and growling deep inside it chest. The growling seemed to echo all around him and Anthony knew why: the growls were coming from each of the three heads. Three times the growls.

But it was the flaming eyes that held him transfixed. Heck, he could even see the black smoke rising up from the eyes, trailing behind each head.

It was then—right about then, anyway—that Anthony decided he was dreaming. That there was just no way in hell any of this was real. And, if he was dreaming, he might as well just close his eyes, and wait to wake up.

Which was exactly what he did, even as the floor beneath him shook with each of the creature's steps...

***

The nightmare—and Anthony had very nearly convinced himself that this was indeed one long, horrific nightmare—had started all the way back in math class, with Mr. Matthews.

The math teacher had been acting very strange today, sweating and drinking lots of water and acting, well, erratic. Anthony wasn't a hundred percent sure what *erratic* meant, but the word somehow fit his math teacher's behavior.

At one point, he'd caught the smallish man staring openly at him. In the past, Mr. Matthews would quickly look away, but this time, he hadn't. This time, he kept staring and staring, and Anthony had begun to feel uncomfortable. Yes, he was used to kids staring at him at school, where he was known as a major freak by one and all, but rarely by adults. And when Mr. Matthews did finally look away, Anthony couldn't help but notice the small smile on the man's thin lips.

And the day went downhill from there.

Worst day ever, he thought, keeping his eyes closed. *C'mon, Anthony. Wake up, buddy. No way this is happening. No way you are shackled to a chair in a dirty old forgotten warehouse, with four silver-tipped arrows sticking out of you, and with this... this thing coming at you...*

"No way," he whispered. "No way..."

Except he didn't feel like he was dreaming. Mostly because he had never been in so much pain before. Unless he was dreaming about the pain, too. Was that possible?

He didn't know. He didn't know what was possible anymore and what wasn't anymore. Everything he did seemed impossible. Everything his mom did seemed impossible, too. Even his stupid sister was a big weirdo, reading everyone's minds like a freakazoid.

He closed his eyes tighter, felt the tears squeeze out. The pain in his stomach was terrible. The more he gasped and struggled, the more the sticky warmth flowed from the wound, pooling in his lap. And the more the arrow seemed to grate against his spine.

But he kept them closed, even as he felt the hot breath on his face.

The hot, putrid breath.

***

Anthony would never, ever forgive himself if he pissed himself.

He didn't know why that was so important to him, but it was. Babies pissed themselves. Not men. Or brave boys. And he was a brave boy. His mother had told him that all the time. And he felt it, too, deep in his core. He was a brave boy, and he wasn't going to let anything scare him. Not these freaks who tied him up, and not this three-headed freaky monster dog either.

And he sure as hell wasn't going to piss himself.

Anthony knew that the world he lived in was getting stranger by the minute. He was proof of it. His mother was proof of it, too. So were Kingsley and Allison and his sister. That in this same, weird world could also be a three-headed devil dog, was somehow harder for him to believe. But the more he felt its stinking hot breath, the more he believed it.

Maybe, just maybe, if he kept his eyes closed, it would go away. Maybe there was even a chance it would disappear altogether. Anthony held out hope.

Now, he felt something wet on his cheek. Something wet and bulbous and warm. A dog's nose. It had had grazed his skin. But it hadn't been cold like almost every other dog's nose he'd felt. This was warm. Hot even. No, burning!

The pain finally drove him to open his eyes, which he regretted immediately.

The creature—or creatures—were just inches from Anthony's face. One directly in front of him, its eyes burning, lapping tongues of flame. How the creature could actually *see*, Anthony didn't know. The other two heads hovered just above Anthony's shoulders, their own eyes spitting flames and emitting curling fingers of black smoke.

It doesn't see me, Anthony suddenly thought, watching again as the creature moved its many heads this way and that. Indeed, Anthony was suddenly sure that the creature—or creatures— might be blind. Yes, it was the way the three heads were swaying, like three cobras at the command of an Indian flute player.

If they wanted Anthony, they had him dead to rights. Anthony wasn't going anywhere, couldn't go anywhere. And yet, the heads continued to bob and sway, their noses sniffing, snouts crinkling. It seemed to be looking for something, something that wasn't Anthony.

Anthony was suddenly sure of something... the dogs were having a tough time of it. He sensed their frustration. Whatever they were looking for, they weren't finding it.

Indeed, the flames in their eye sockets spat higher, rising clear above them. Three sets of twin flames that were absolute proof that monsters were real.

He was now only vaguely aware of the tears on his cheeks. He'd been silently crying for a few minutes now. Crying was fine, he told himself. He could cry, just as long as he didn't piss himself...

It was then that Anthony heard the footsteps approaching slowly, from roughly the same direction the dog had appeared. Whoever was coming was wearing boots.

And from within the shadows—just beyond the reach of the dusty bulb, he saw a man coming, a man with red, glowing eyes.

***

"Down boy," said the man from across the room who then stepped out into the dim light.

The dog growled—or, rather, one of the damned heads did—but moved aside. And as the man walked toward them, Anthony wondered who on earth would approach a three-headed dog. Anthony didn't know, but the man wasn't scared. He passed into the light with smooth confidence, his boots tapping. The man was tall and lean—but muscular, too. Now, Anthony saw all the tattoos along the man's arms. One tattoo in particular caught the boy's attention: a scaly dragon that wound around and around the man's right forearm, a dragon that looked so... damn... real.

Now the man stopped in front of Anthony and crossed his arms over his chest, and cocked his head to one side. Unlike the dogs and their fire eyes, this man's eyes glowed softly. Still damn creepy, though. Anthony had seen Kingsley's eyes glow like this. But Kingsley's were yellow. Amber, he'd heard his mother once say. Once or twice, he had even caught his own mother's eyes glowing.

We're all freaks, Anthony thought.

"Well, well..." began the man, and as he spoke, his lips slowly curled into the wickedest grin Anthony had ever seen. "And what sort of freak are you?"

Chapter 24

Having the key to the kingdom was one thing. Knowing which door to open was quite another.

Now, as I swiped through Mr. Matthews' tablet computer, randomly pressing apps and opening his web browser, I was beginning to realize how futile all this might be. Over time, the contents of the tablet could be pored over and disseminated and cataloged. But now, with the sun setting in just over an hour, the many apps on the tablet proved a daunting and frightening prospect.

Where to look? What to look *for*? I didn't know, but I did know the tablet computer was key. I felt it to the very core of my being. I just knew it. I just didn't know why or where to look.

Kingsley paced the small living room, its floorboards sagging and creaking under his weight. He was running his hands through his thick mane, sometimes pulling at the hair. Sometimes, he grunted. Each time, Sherbet snapped his head around and looked at him. No doubt, the older detective had long since picked up from me that my boyfriend was going through a change, a metamorphosis of frightening proportions. Literally. In just under an hour, my boyfriend would cease to exist, and a real monster would be standing in his place. A mindless, hungry, terrible thing to behold.

Jesus, Sam, came Sherbet's thoughts. *They did not talk about this in the police academy.*

Maybe they should, I replied.

Earlier, after a heated, private discussion between us in the other room, Kingsley had called Franklin, giving him our address. In our one-on-one, Kingsley had said, "Wherever it is, I'm going in. I'll battle them all to protect your son."

"No, Kingsley. You'll be killed by the pack."

"Anthony's a part of you. That means I'm willing to give my life for his." His amber eyes were intent on mine and I could hear his brave heart hammering in his massive chest. At that moment, I had never loved Kingsley more.

"I won't let you be killed by them. Call for a ride home. Now. I mean it."

Kingsley had reluctantly done as I'd asked. After the call, he'd said, "I want to tear him to pieces, Sam. I want to tear them all to pieces for taking your son."

I knew Franklin the faithful butler would be here soon, and so did Sherbet. Truthfully, I had never seen Kingsley change—only the early stages. What I had seen wasn't pretty, and it wasn't that far off, either. Franklin had better get here soon. *Very soon.*

My fear grew as the minutes clicked by. In a cold sweat, I desperately swiped and clicked on apps. I had long since gone through his email, but nothing seemed promising. Indeed, it was mostly cluttered with computer ads. I suspected the email attached to the tablet wasn't his main account. A junk account he used when ordering off the Internet.

Another app, the logo a purplish "N" imprinted on an open folder, was an app I wasn't familiar with —but the moment I pushed it, I knew how right it felt, and my heart leaped.

As I waited for the app to open, Kingsley paced faster and faster, and now, ran both hands through his hair, really pulling it. His heavy breathing had morphed into deep-throated growls. Sherbet kept his hand near his holstered firearm. I didn't blame him.

The tablet's screen kicked me over to a page filled with file headers. Hundreds and hundreds of file headers. Turned out, this was a Microsoft app for storing notes on the cloud. And Matthews had stored a crap-ton of notes.

Too many, I thought, panicking. *Too many! I would never have time to go through them all!*

More tears sprung to my eyes as I scanned the list: "Bills"; "Morning Schedule"; "Dream Vacations"; "Credit Cards"; "All-Time Baseball

Team"; "All-Time Football Team"; "Movies to Watch" and so on and so on.

And fucking so on...

Nothing about werewolves, or his association with a very bad man, or what they intended to do with my son.

It was then that I knew I couldn't save my son. At least, not on my own. There were just too many files... and how could I even trust my own psychic hit? And since when was I psychic anyway?

I hadn't been, not really, not ever.

Now, I stood and ran my own clawed fingers through my own thick hair. I stood there, staring down at the tablet, and realized there wasn't going to be enough time. I wasn't going to find my son. There was no hope, no chance. Most certainly, there was no way I could go through these hundreds of file folders in time.

I looked at my cell. Just under an hour before sundown. An hour until a vanload of animals were going to potentially descend upon my son. My son with his magical blood. Had my son been a full vampire, the werewolves would not have seen his aura. His aura would have been hidden to him, to everyone. But my son was something in-between— and they could see it, which had left him exposed to the likes of them and others. And if it hadn't been this group, it would have been another, and another. Other Light Warriors banded together, lived together, trained and fought together. That is, those who lived to see adulthood. Others were watched continuously, throughout their lives, as was the case with my family and, undoubtedly, many families like mine.

We had assumed my superhero thirteen-year-old son would be okay on his own. I had assumed it. It was easy to think that. Hell, he had nearly defeated five full-ass grown men on his own. Men with supernatural strength. But five werewolves would be different. My son wouldn't stand a chance. And now, no one—but no one—knew where he was, and all these stupid fucking files on this stupid fucking tablet were of no help at all.

For the first time, perhaps in all my life, I felt completely useless, completely at a loss, and completely without hope.

It was at that moment that the front door slammed open, and Allison and Tammy spilled inside the house, to Sherbet's dismay. They ignored his protests regarding protocol.

"Give me the tablet, Sam," said Allison. "I know where to look. And for God's sake, would someone give her a hug?"

Chapter 25

The smile on the stranger's face widened, stretching almost painfully from ear to ear.

If not for the smile, the guy would have looked kind of normal. Maybe like a greaser from those movies Mommy and Aunt Mary Lou were always watching. The man stopped a few feet away from him, and now, Anthony could smell the sweat on him.

The man circled Anthony, his glowing eyes seemingly taking everything in. "What am I to make of this? Why has my venerable hound led me here, to this place? To you? A boy shackled to a chair, over a floor drain that's not quite a drain. A drain that leads to a blood-stained receptacle. All while nine werewolves wait in the next room over, werewolves in various degrees of transformation, werewolves whose minds are closed to me, but, I suspect, are planning on some very, very bad things."

Anthony was pretty sure the man with the fire eyes wasn't expecting an answer from him. He also didn't know what a receptacle was, but that was probably okay. A lot of the words coming out of the man were kinda terrible. It was okay if he didn't know what one or two of them meant.

Still, something inside Anthony—something rebellious, perhaps—decided to offer an answer anyway. "Maybe you came to help me?"

The man threw back his head and Anthony was certain he was about to hear a burst of laughter; instead, the man stood straight again, perhaps thinking better of giving away his presence to a pack of nine werewolves.

"Help? Ah, lad, I haven't helped anyone for a long time. Maybe never."

"Why not?"

"Let's just say... it's not in my nature."

Anthony shrugged, although shrugging kind of hurt. Anthony didn't see what the big deal was in helping him. At least, call the police. But he let that idea slip away. After all, the man before definitely did not project a helping vibe. If anything, he projected a mean vibe, a cruel vibe, an angry vibe. Anthony decided he liked the word: *vibe*.

The man walked around completely, his boots clicking lightly on the cement floor. "I can see your aura, yet, I do not have access to your mind. Very strange indeed. Tell me, do you hear voices in your head? Voices that sound exactly like your dad? Almost as if he's there with you? Inside of you? Guiding you?"

Anthony didn't know what to say or how to respond. Yes, he had heard his father's voice, but only recently, and he liked hearing it so very much that it hurt.

"Did you think you were going crazy?"

Anthony hadn't thought that. The voice was soothing and helpful. But it was so deep down inside that not even Tammy with her super telepathy could hear it. In fact, for the longest time, Anthony had ignored it. He just simply smiled when he heard it, but didn't make anything of it. In that way, he was certain it had escaped Tammy's attention, who seemed to hear everything, all the time. God, she was such a weirdo!

"Or were you happy to hear him again? Your father, I mean. Tell me, why did my pet lead me here, to this place, to you now?"

"I don't know," said Anthony. "Why don't you ask one of its stupid heads?"

Anthony thought that was funny, but the man before him apparently didn't. The man's once-creepy smile had descended down into a fierce scowl, pulling at the corners of his lips. Anthony was reminded of the theater masks that represented comedy and drama.

The man paused and cocked his head, and Anthony heard it now, too. The scratching of something... perhaps claws. Lots of scratching.

Anthony also heard moaning and growls and howls.

"They are turning, boy, and they are coming for you. I suspect you are to be their sport. If you could see what I could see, you would understand why."

Anthony couldn't see his own aura. In fact, he had only barely begun seeing a light glow around some people, but not anything that was very clear. But he knew that his family sported a silver dragon within their auras—at least, he and his sister did, and maybe even Aunt Mary Lou and her kids.

"I know about the silver serpent," said Anthony.

"Do you, now? Then do you know that the men in the next room—men who are in various degrees of transformation—are planning to consume you completely, toenails and all?"

Okay, Anthony hadn't known that, not really. He had mostly ignored why he had been locked to a chair, over a drain, in an abandoned warehouse. But, of course, the man's words made sense.

"You may not be scared now, boy. But you should be. So should the vile creature hiding inside you."

Anthony wasn't sure what the man was talking about. Vile creature? What was hiding inside him? Was the man somehow talking about his father? Was his father hiding inside him?

"Ah, I can see the realization dawning on you, boy. So, you *have* heard the voices."

"My father?"

"Very good, boy. He has been running for a

long, long time. But I think we have him cornered and, if my guess is right, in a few short minutes, he won't be hiding anymore."

His father was hiding inside him? *Inside him?* Anthony didn't know what to make of this new information—and the scrabbling of claws in the room next door made it almost impossible to think.

Was *that* why he'd been hearing his father's voice? It hadn't been just his imagination? And how the hell did his father get inside him? And why? And why the hell was Anthony even listening to this crazy man in front of him?

"Ah, I see I've hit a nerve. You've heard him, then, whispering in your ear, or from down deep in your mind. Your father... he's not a bad man by my standards. But I want him like I want all men. You see, I went to a lot of trouble creating his special version of hell, and I intend to drag him there, one way or another."

Anthony blinked. Wait, what? His father's own special version of hell? What the hell did that mean, no pun intended. Anthony nearly grinned at his own joke. But he didn't, couldn't. What was happening here? He looked again at the man with the glowing eyes, the man with what looked like a living tattoo. The man with a pet dog with three heads. The man talking about "creating" hell.

No, Anthony thought. *No freakin' way.*

The man before him continued... that is, if he was a man at all. "But Daniel Moon chose instead to hide in his own boy. A coward's move, of course.

Then again, you are a very special boy, I see. Yes... very, very special." The man before him paused. "I could have use for a boy like you."

"Leave me alone," said Anthony. "And leave my daddy alone, too."

"I might just do that, boy. I might just do exactly that. But first—"

And here, the devil—yes, Anthony was sure the man was the devil—snaked out a hand and grabbed hold of the arrow in Anthony's shoulder. Anthony gasped. Just touching it hurt.

"—let's level the playing field a bit, shall we?"

Anthony was just puzzling over the meaning of "leveling the playing field" when the devil ripped free the arrow in Anthony's shoulder. Anthony saw white, then red, and cried out as liquid warmth flowed down his bicep. That hurt far worse than he was prepared for. Maybe the silver had affected him. He didn't know.

The devil did the same with the three remaining arrow, pulling each out in unison—and with reckless abandon. Perhaps even glee. The one that had hurt most of all—the one in his stomach—also provided him the greatest relief when removed. Anthony had cried out the loudest with that one, not caring if the werewolves next door heard him, especially since they were making a bigger racket.

With a clatter, the devil tossed aside the bloodied arrow, and stood tall over Anthony. If anything, the devil seemed disappointed there hadn't been more arrows to pull free. Anthony felt his eyes on him. "You are already healing, boy. Good, good."

Anthony felt it, too. He felt the wounds closing, felt his insides moving, stitching together, somehow. He also felt himself getting stronger, too.

"I guess you were wrong," said Anthony, now that he had unclenched his teeth enough to talk.

"Wrong about what, boy?"

"The devil does help."

The man before him opened his mouth to speak, but then, closed it again. Finally, he leaned down and stuck his handsome face just inches from Anthony. "You are a clever boy. But I want you to remember one thing if you make it out of here alive, which I doubt you will."

Anthony wasn't afraid. Heck, did the devil even know that Samantha Moon was his mom? He said, "What?"

The man with the glowing eyes—a man who was not a man—leaned down and whispered into Anthony's ear: "I want you to remember who really helped you in your hour of greatest need."

With that, the devil stepped back and snapped his fingers and two things happened at the same time—maybe even three or four:

The cuffs at his wrists and feet sprang open...

The devil and his three-headed dog disappeared...

And somewhere, Anthony heard a door creak open...

Chapter 26

"You two really aren't supposed to be in here —" said Sherbet, then caught sight of my look— and Allison's look, and even Tammy's own scathing look of utter contempt that only a teenager could give. He threw up his hands. "Ah, geez, never mind. Welcome to the party."

Searching for clues to my kidnapped son's whereabouts hardly seemed like a party—but I knew the detective meant well. We were all at our wit's end, and we literally had a ticking time bomb to contend with. A time bomb in the form of the setting sun.

My daughter summed up my thoughts nicely: "Worst. Party. Ever. Like I really want to be in this creep's house."

Allison, meanwhile, was frowning at the tablet, her face and big brown eyes aglow. As she scrolled through the subject headers, she said, "I've been waiting for a psychic hit on your son, Sam. Been waiting for it ever since we heard the bad news." She continued scrolling through the many, many headers. "As you know, I have no control over my hits. Sometimes, they never come. It would be nice if a picture of the warehouse where they took your son—"

"Why did you say, 'warehouse'?"

"Did I say, 'warehouse'?"

"You did, yes."

"Interesting. I didn't mean to say, 'warehouse.' It just sort of slipped out."

"*Interesting* doesn't help find my son. It's either a warehouse or it's not—"

"Easy, Sam," said Sherbet. "We'll figure it out..."

I paced in a tight circle. I didn't know what to do with my hands, so, I shook them in front of me. Snapping at Allison did no good at all, and probably stopped up what psychic hits she was getting. "Sorry," I said to no one in particular.

"It's okay," said Allison. "Anyway, we had been following your train of thoughts from out in the van... and the moment you pulled up the OneNote app, I got the hit I'd been waiting for."

Except now, she looked as perplexed as I was sure I'd looked, when I had been scanning the myriad of headers. It was all I could do to not throw the couch against the far wall, which I could totally do.

Allison was biting her lower lip; a sure sign she was in "psychic receiving mode." Most people didn't realize that biting their lower lip triggered an easier flow of psychic hits. It's why so many people did it, and it actually worked. Allison didn't bother looking up at me when she answered my unspoken telepathic concern, "I'm seeing letters and numbers, Sam. It's a pattern I have to unlock."

"And it has to do with his OneNote files?" I asked.

"It does. But this is gonna take me a minute or two."

I had just decided I would spend that minute or two pulling all my hair out, when a vehicle came to a screeching halt outside.

Chapter 27

In a blink, Anthony was up and out of his chair.
He dashed away from the scraping, clawing, growling that was coming from the nearby room—away from where he had heard the door open. He held his breath as he ran, and made sure his feet were quiet, too. Like the way Indians supposedly ran.

He found himself at the far end of the warehouse. Unfortunately, the light from the single bulb didn't really reach this far. Still, there was enough of it to see there were no windows or doors on this end. Nothing higher up either, except for dirty rafters. Anthony was beginning to think that nothing was supposed to get out of here. Or in here, either.

It was looking more and more like the way out was where all the noise was coming from, where the men were turning into werewolves. At least, that's what Anthony imagined they were doing. Why they were all in one room, he didn't know. But it was like a locker room.

Maybe he couldn't run... but he could hide, right?

Yes, he could hide.

That is, until he remembered that hiding from a pack of werewolves might be impossible. After all, Kingsley could smell a fart, like, a mile away. Anthony liked that about Kingsley.

As he considered his options—which really seemed too few, he felt—Anthony heard the sound of metal clanging. It sounded... yes, it sounded like a metal door opening and closing. And rattling, too. Like a cage door, maybe.

An engine started. Followed by the sound of a pneumatic lift being engaged. Anthony knew the sound. He'd walked past enough construction sites, heard them on TV, and seen them in his video games. It was the sound of a forklift... or maybe even something bigger.

Like a moth drawn to a flame—he'd heard that expression a few times—he felt himself drawn to the noise of the smoothly humming engine, an engine that vibrated the very floor beneath his feet. He saw the torture chair—as he had started to think of it—and the single light bulb above. Anthony crept around stacks of crates and boxes, down a row of racks that reached all the way up into the inky blackness. He crouched behind a dusty old machine of some sort. It smelled of dirt and old oil.

His instincts told him he was well-hidden, but he knew well-hidden meant nothing to a werewolf, especially a pack of them. A pack that was getting closer to transforming somewhere on the other side of that dusty light bulb.

Yes, they could sniff him out, but they still had to catch him, and Anthony could climb with the best of them. Better than the best of them, and this place was zigzagged with crossbeams and rafters and lofts.

The pneumatic engine stopped, and the sudden silence was unnerving. Anthony didn't dare move or breathe from behind his box. Now, from above, he heard more creaking and rattling. Something was above. No, someone was above.

Whatever or whoever it was, Anthony didn't know—but he could guess. After all, Anthony was 99% sure his math teacher wasn't a werewolf. Or a vampire either.

It's Mr. Matthews, he thought. *He's above me... watching.*

A second or two later, all the lights in the warehouse turned on at once.

Chapter 28

There were four of them. Monsters, that is.

Franklin was with three of the more cognizant of Lichtenstein's creations, all of whom had been liberated from the very castle that Dracula now called home.

Another story, another time...

A half-dozen of the creatures had been adopted, as it were, by Kingsley, all of whom now lived on his property, many in his guest house out back, to be exact. Which might explain why Kingsley spent a lot of time at my place these days. Anyway, his six new houseguests were all hulking and some grotesquely misshapen. When Lichtenstein had assembled his monsters from stolen corpses, he did so with an eye toward usefulness, and not aesthetics. Now, they gardened for Kingsley, cooked for him, cleaned for him. One was adept at mechanical work, and kept all of Kingsley's vehicles—five of them, to be exact—in superb working order. Perhaps most important, all were now bonded to Kingsley, perhaps not to the extent they had been with their original creator, a man who had been exiled far, far away from here. But they were bonded to Kingsley, nonetheless. I wasn't entirely sure how I felt about that.

At present, only the gangly, long-limbed Franklin entered the home. The other three remained in the front yard, standing mostly still, awaiting orders. One of them had an ugly scar that wrapped entirely around his forehead. At some point in his life, he had received a new brain.

Franklin had rushed immediately to Kingsley, no doubt seeing the advanced stage of transitioning his master was in. Yes, he used words like 'master' and meant it, too. If Kingsley ever thought I was going to call him master, he had another thing coming. The least of which would be my foot up his hairy ass.

With the arrival of Franklin, Sherbet mumbled something about, "The more, the merrier," as he'd long since kissed away the legality of this search warrant. Any evidence gathered here now was as good as tainted.

In no uncertain terms, Franklin let us know that Master Kingsley needed to leave now, but that he had brought three of his strongest brothers with him, to use as we saw fit. He'd said brothers, not me. And, yeah, I knew Kingsley felt a kinship with all the Lichtenstein monsters. Apparently, so did Tammy who, amazingly, hadn't taken her eyes off one of them... a younger-looking monster who, if you removed the fact that he sported a face that appeared to have been sewn on by someone partially blind, did look kind of handsome. That is, if you didn't mind a guy's face being sewn on and all. Which, apparently, she didn't.

Your brother is still missing, young lady, I thought to her, loud and clear.

She squeaked and turned all sorts of shades of red.

Worse, I think the young-looking monster just might have caught her eye in return.

Lord help us all.

Anyway, we were told that each of the Lichtenstein monsters had been armed with a silver dagger—and each knew exactly what to do with it. I knew that Franklin and his "brothers" were far stronger than Kingsley in his *human* form. How much stronger—if at all—they were to fully formed werewolves, I didn't know.

"Found it!" said Allison triumphantly, just as Franklin had gotten Kingsley to the door. Although neither as tall nor thick as Kingsley, Franklin manhandled the hairy bastard easily enough.

She quickly explained that she had been seeing a series of letters and words, and soon realized they were the corresponding letters and words to a series of files within files. Once she'd found the first file, she moved on to the next letter and word, and so and so on until she had come across a single file called *Mockingbird*.

Kingsley had Franklin wait at the door as Allison read from the file, and what a sordid, terrible, horror-filled file it was. In it, Matthews described his continuous search among his students for children who displayed the "mark," as he called it. To date, he'd found only one other student with it —and Matthews had been richly rewarded. Even better, he'd been granted access to the feeding. This was, apparently, a highlight to his life, watching an innocent child with the mark being rendered to pieces by the local pack of werewolves. Matthews hadn't given names, but I was willing to bet he'd been describing the murder of the child who had gone missing three years prior.

"I understand," said Allison, "but I don't understand, either. What's going on here?"

"Matthews is a scout," said Kingsley. "A human who can see auras."

Allison said, "But he's a teacher..."

"Which gives him access to children and their auras. In particular..." He stopped talking, grimacing, hanging on to Franklin, who didn't seem happy about any of this. Then again, Franklin didn't seem happy even when he seemed happy.

"In particular *what*?" asked Allison.

But it was Tammy who stepped forward, Tammy who had access to everyone's mind in the small house, including Kingsley's. "In particular, children who display my family's mark."

"Children," I added, "who have not yet found protection from the Alchemist and the Light Warriors."

My own son fell somewhere between all of that. Without a guardian angel, he was already susceptible to attack. Without the light worker's protection, he was vulnerable as well. His own great strength had made him seem beyond harm. I had taken it for granted. I should have been there to pick him up, every day, until I was certain he was safe or could take care of himself.

There was no time for blame. There was only finding my son... and finding him *now*.

"He mentions The Row in Carson," said Allison, having scanned the notes.

"The Row is an industrial park in Carson," said Sherbet. "Mostly, it's a long street of warehouses."

I looked at Allison; she looked at me. I said to her, "Does he say which warehouse?"

"No, Sam. I'm sorry."

But I was already moving through the house and out into the waning light of day. We had, if anything, twenty minutes before full sunset.

Chapter 29

Anthony shielded his eyes.

From his position behind the old machine, Anthony could barely believe what he was seeing: Hanging from a metal cage, and standing behind what appeared to be a sort of makeshift control panel, was none other than his eighth-grade algebra teacher, Mr. Matthews. The whole thing was suspended from a cable, supported by an indoor crane. Anthony nearly stepped out from behind his hiding place and asked his teacher what the hell was going on. That is, until Anthony saw the gleeful look in his math teacher's eyes. Not just gleeful... but insane.

Anthony was pretty sure he had never seen such a look on anyone's face, like ever. Maybe in the movies. But no one acted this insane, this wicked in real life, did they?

Anthony wasn't sure what to make of that, or what to do with that information, other than never, ever enroll in another one of Mr. Matthews' classes. Like ever again.

And what was the deal with the swinging cage, like a hundred feet above the floor? Anthony didn't know exactly how high up the cage was, but it felt like a hundred feet; either way, it was way up there, near the ceiling and lights. Where Mr. Matthews would be safe from the werewolves, no doubt. Werewolves that were even now howling in the nearby room. For some reason, the words "staging room" popped into Anthony's mind. Maybe that was what the room was called. Anthony didn't know.

"Come out, come out, wherever you are, little Moon," said the familiar voice of his math teacher. What wasn't familiar, though, was the gleeful, high-pitch, sing-song quality to the voice.

There was, like, no way Anthony was coming out, and from where he hid behind the machine, he was certain his weirdo teacher couldn't see him, either. No, the only thing that was gonna get Anthony moving was a pack of werewolves, and the longer they stayed behind that door, the better. Speaking of which, from his position, he thought he could see a row of offices in the far distance. At least, he saw some darkened windows. Was it a way out?

"I went to a lot of trouble to arrange for you to be here, tonight. Oh, the planning, the preparations, the coordinating. The precautions. All in place, and all so that my hungry friends can feed. And all so that I could watch from above.

"You see, my friends you can forgive. They are just a pack of wild animals. At least, they will be in a few minutes. A minute and forty-eight seconds, to be exact. Anyway, it's me who is the real monster here. Me, who coordinated all of this, including the renovation of this building. You could say it's now werewolf-proof. Most important, it's sound-proof."

Anthony swallowed, shaking his head. Who knew that Mr. Matthews was such a sicko? He certainly didn't. As far as he knew, his sister had never taken a course from Matthews. If she had, she would have undoubtedly dipped into his mind and seen what a freak he was.

"I always knew I was different," Matthews was saying, sounding almost nostalgic. "I could always see the light around a body. I could always tell, for instance, if someone was sick, or had a disease, or were going to die. I could always tell when a person was particularly happy, too, or particularly saintly, for lack of a better word. Those people were always so bright, so beautiful. But, occasionally, I would come across those who did not give off an aura of any kind, those who seemed different, fiercer, wilder.

"It wouldn't be long before I would come to understand that such people—such creatures—were werewolves. I ingratiated myself with them, became friends with them, and soon worked for them. After all, I also see others, too. Those who have a special mark, if you will. Those who sport the silver serpent. Like Angie Sanderson a few years ago, and like you now. Turns out the werewolves have quite a thing for the silver serpent, quite a hunger, if you will. From what I understand, those such as yourself and Angie, make the hulking beasts even stronger, more formidable, and give them extra life. Yes, *life*. Didn't you know that? By consuming your blood, they can live longer. Unlike their vampiric friends —like your mother, for instance, and, yes, I know what she is—who are given immortality, werewolves have a set lifespan. Granted, the lifespan is far, far longer than most mortals, sometimes two or three times longer. But consuming one of the marked... *oh,* they can add dozens of years to their lives! Many, many dozens."

Anthony didn't know that. Granted, he didn't know much about any of this—including what, exactly, he was. Sometimes, his sister told him things—things she'd gleaned from their mother's mind, or Kingsley's mind. Sometimes, his mom told him things, too. And there was even the occasional time he overheard things, like when Mommy and Kingsley were talking late into the night. But he hadn't known his blood was *so* special.

"I have been ever watchful for the mark. Sadly, not as common as one would think. But then, lo, our school was fortunate enough to have two in one year! Tammy Moon and Angie Sanderson. Ooh, who would I choose? Turned out, Angie was in my class and walked home alone each day and seemed an easier target. But your mother had a nasty habit of picking up Tammy each day. But I saw you, often waiting in the van, and I saw your mom, too. And her own lack of an aura. Such a weird, glorious family. And I knew you would be coming up in a few years from the elementary school. I could wait, I could wait. Besides, yes, I needed the dust to settle after Angie. And I picked her. Oh, yes. I picked her, and I watched my adopted brothers consume her completely and totally.

"And then you came up through the system, but you were... so different. Not like the other boys at all. Stronger, faster, scarier. The werewolves were not pleased. This was not what they'd signed up for. You were an unknown, but they were also hungry for more blood. So... damn... hungry. And so, we staged a coup of sorts. The plan today was to have taken your mother as well."

Anthony didn't know what a "coo" was, but he kept listening.

"After all, they had a bone to pick with her. There was a rumor among them that she was responsible for the deaths of some in their pack, those who were killed in the mountains of Arrowhead a few years ago. The werewolves were confident they could overcome your mother, although her own unusual gifts concerned them. How could she exist easily in the daylight? Surely she was a vampire. But she was an unknown, too. Either way, their hunger had reached a tipping point. They were willing to be reckless. Maybe I was, too. This was all so exciting... and bloody.

"But then there you were, alone and waiting—and now, here we are, in my *ware*house of horror, you could say. You see, when I'm not feeding my boys the marked children, I am feeding them other things. They prefer the living, and so, this warehouse has seen its fair share of lambs and goats and cows. I am a regular customer, you could say, of the local farms. After all, I pay top dollar for their doomed creatures."

Anthony was getting tired of hearing his creepy teacher, and wished he had his BB gun. Anthony was always a good shot. He was certain he could nail his teacher through the bars of the cage.

"I paid top dollar to construct this hovering command center, if you will. From here, I can control the lights. More importantly, I can control the door to the staging room—"

Anthony had known it was called the staging room. He nearly pumped his fist in the darkness.

But Matthews was already blabbing on: "Because no one—but no one—wants to be down there when the werewolves are unleashed. It's terrible to see, even from up here. The power, the speed, the anger. It's all very supernatural and not of this world. Were they better climbers, I would surely have fallen victim by now. But the dumb brutes never think to look up. And so, I watch them from above, orchestrating their release, the lights, and their food.

"Which is why I pity you, little boy. I will pity you, even while I'll watch them devour you, tearing you limb from limb, piece by piece, blood and bones and hair and nails."

Anthony had had enough. From a nearby shelf, he spotted a rusted screw. He snatched it, took aim, and launched it as hard as he could from between the dusty rows, up and out, a laser shot if ever he had seen one. He didn't hit his math teacher, but the explosion of metal against metal shocked the little man into silence.

And, really, that was all Anthony could ask for. Well, maybe a little more. A small window to shimmy through would work.

When the little teacher had recovered, Anthony watched him check his watch, then nod—and then push a lever. Anthony was pretty certain his math teacher was an evil genius. Either that, or the man had seen too many Marvel movies.

A sharp clack of metal against metal echoed through the massive warehouse. Anthony was certain it sounded exactly like a deadbolt sliding open.

Anthony swallowed and watched as his third-period math teacher next pulled on what looked like night-vision goggles. Any kid who had ever played Halo would recognize the goggles.

With that, Matthews flipped another switch—and the lights went out, including the dusty bulb above the torture chair. Or would it be considered the feeding chair? Anthony didn't know, but either way, he shuddered. The row of offices in the far distance now seemed impossible to find in complete darkness.

"The beasties don't like the light, as you can imagine," said Mr. Matthews from way up high, his voice coming out of the darkness. "Besides, they don't need it."

Anthony was certain he heard the sound of claws against the concrete floor. This time, the sound wasn't coming from behind a closed door. This time, the sounds were out in the open, and they were coming at him.

Fast.

Chapter 30

There were six of us in my minivan. Three Lichtenstein monsters, myself, Allison, and Tammy. Allison was wedged in the back, between the monsters, one of whom was sitting in the foldout seat in the very, very back. I could have been a mad mom in a minivan, bringing her van full of freaks to a Little League practice. Behind us, Sherbet followed, although he kept his siren and flasher silent at my request.

As I tore down the road, I gave Tammy a mental snapshot of what I had in mind, and she nodded at me from the front seat.

"I can do it, Mommy," she said. "I've done it before. Or something like it."

Admittedly, I was struck that she had called me, "Mommy." A first for her in many years.

"Good," I said. "Good."

And we drove down, the sun inched closer and closer to the horizon, all while I nearly crawled out of my skin.

"You okay, Sam?" asked Allison from the back seat.

"No," I said. "No, I'm not."

***

The arrows, Anthony!

Anthony heard the words clearly, and it spurred him into action, even before he had really thought about what to do. He was now absolutely certain he'd been hearing his dad's voice these past few months—and now, this time, the voice was as loud as ever.

Anthony dashed forward through the dark, relieved that he had seen his surroundings in light, even if briefly. Now, relying on memory, he rushed toward where he knew the torture chair sat bolted to the floor—

He cleared the row of shelving and sensed he was in open space. The chair would be before him, even while his crazy math teacher hung above him, no doubt watching his every move through the night-vision goggles.

Mom is sooooo going to kick his ass, thought Anthony, as he nearly ran headlong into the chair. Luckily, a zigzagging flare of white light had raced across his vision, briefly illuminating the chair. Anthony saw these zigzagging flares of light sometimes. Now, he wished he could see them more often, because they really did light up the area around them. But this flare came and went quickly.

In darkness, he dropped to his knees, and felt with his hands until he had discovered three of the four arrows that the devil had pulled out of him. Now he had weapons. And then, he was running again, scrabbling, slipping and falling in his haste, catching himself with his hands. He'd felt the rumbling from the cement, rumbling of many running feet—and heard the clacking of claws.

Now, as he peered from behind a row of nearby shelves, he saw the glowing amber eyes from across the empty space. No doubt, the creatures were only now realizing their prey had escaped. Anthony doubted the creepy Matthews would say anything. Matthews had made it clear that he preferred to remain anonymously high above, safe from the creatures. Watching like the world's biggest creep.

Anthony knew, from his limited conversations with Kingsley, that werewolves were sort of mindless once transformed. Like true animals. Or true monsters. There was no reasoning with them, or running from them, or fighting them. Or in this case, hiding from them.

Which is why Anthony had quit breathing altogether. And quit moving, too. He was even certain his heartbeat had stopped, too, if that was possible. But maybe that was just his imagination.

Anthony watched the amber eyes fill the open space where he had sat shackled, waiting to be feasted upon. As they gathered, Anthony sensed something else, too. A darkness, an evil. It hit him in waves and seemed to fill the massive warehouse.

A flash of zigzagging light. Nothing he hadn't seen before, but it moved through the room and between the creatures. Okay, now *those* he hadn't seen before. Ever. Try as he might to imagine Kingsley a howling werewolf each full moon, nothing came close to seeing the real deal in person. In this case, many real deals.

Anthony was ill-prepared for just how massive the creatures were, how hulking and damn scary they looked. For the first time all night, Anthony knew real fear. Terrible, gut-clenching, blood-freezing fear that made him want to hide behind the crate and curl into a tight ball and pray and cry and wish like crazy that his mommy was here.

He did none of that, except to stay where he was, holding his breath, sweating, and fighting now an urge to run somewhere, anywhere. And maybe—just maybe—fighting an urge to pee his pants.

No dammit. Just no. Please no...

Except there was nowhere to run. No, that wasn't true. The beasties had come out from the holding room. There was a door there. A door controlled by that mad freak Matthews, who probably locked it tight again.

Still, doors could be broken into, couldn't they? Ripped down. Except that the werewolves hadn't ripped it down, which meant it had been some strong door. Maybe too strong even for him.

Another flash of shooting light appeared, and Anthony got another good look at a half-dozen hairy faces—big, wide, hairy faces that looked how he imagined a Bigfoot would look. Except these guys... yes, these guys had snouts? Or were they called muzzles? Anthony wasn't sure. Unlike his mental image of Bigfoot, these guys had a touch of wolf to their appearance.

And the sheer size of them... *holy moly!*

He was certain they were quite a bit taller than Kingsley—at least when Kingsley was in his human form. They were also wider than Kingsley—which was saying something!—and heavily packed with muscle. And so hairy. The blip of light was gone, and the room was plunged once again in total darkness. No, not total. He could still see their yellow eyes.

And now, Anthony heard the one thing he didn't want to hear. Well, that and his own screams of pain. One of them was sniffing the air. And now, the others were following suit. A cacophony of sniffing. How he knew that word, he didn't know, but he could almost imagine their wide nostrils flaring and inhaling his scent. Then he heard something else.

Growling. Low, deep, guttural—and it seemed to come from the biggest sets of lungs he'd ever imagined. A tiger's growl, maybe. Even worse, this wasn't a full-throated growl. It was the growl before the real growl. The build-up growl.

These weren't *beasties*. These were monsters,

and one of them, Anthony was sure, had caught his scent.

An eardrum-shattering, head-splitting howl erupted from seemingly everywhere at once, assaulting Anthony like a physical wave of hate, anger and aggression.

Anthony turned and fled.

Chapter 31

It had been hit or miss there for a few minutes, as I fought the last few rays of light—and as my body transitioned from being weird to super weird.

There were some white-knuckled moments as I gasped and beat the steering wheel and shook my hands and nearly pulled my hair out. What the Lichtenstein monsters thought of me, I didn't know, but the moment passed, and I was better and stronger than I'd ever been before. Maybe ever. Maybe this really was the strongest I had ever been.

I didn't know if the sun affected the Lichtenstein monsters. I did know that different dark masters had different strengths and weaknesses. In the case of the Lichtenstein monsters, I knew they were generally considered to be a lower form of dark master. Dark novices, perhaps. Perhaps the lower down the scale of mastery, the less they were affected by the sun. That is, if they were presently possessed by such entities.

I turned into The Row, and when I had gotten myself under control, I turned to my daughter, and said, "You're on, kiddo."

"I know, Mommy. I've been searching for him this entire time. Geez, give me some credit."

I moved slowly along the mostly quiet street lined with concrete tilt-ups and massive warehouses, all lining both sides of the particularly wide street. Perhaps wide enough for big rigs to make U-turns in. We passed canning businesses, distributors, packing companies. If it got shipped out of Southern California, there was a good likelihood it had originated here, at The Row. Then again, it was going on 6:30 p.m., and many businesses were closed and closing, although the shipping industry never really closed. There was still a smattering of forklift activity, pallets being moved and loaded and unloaded, men and women in brightly-colored vests working in unison. And big rigs. My God, the big rigs. They were parked on streets and in loading docks and moving slowly past us, and parked here, there, and everywhere.

Certainly too much activity for anyone to see anyone pulling up with a child, although if I had to ask each and every person, I would.

Except I didn't have to ask, did I?

I had my secret weapon with me—my own daughter—who even now was projecting her thoughts out and touching upon any and all her mind came into contact with. And not just touching upon, but probing and listening. At least, that was the plan. Whether or not she could find someone hidden from her, or unseen, I didn't know—

"I can, Mom. If they aren't too far away."

I nodded and breathed and fought the urge to give the van more gas. It seemed that Tammy's own gifts were growing exponentially. And I knew she could scan thoughts and hold a conversation at the same time. Boy, did I know that.

As we continued moving down the street, I also somehow resisted the urge to turn into Talos and rip the tops off all the roofs in sight. Casting my own thoughts out did little good, as I could generally only see a few dozen feet around me in any direction, which was barely past the curbs. No, I had to rely solely on my daughter, and maybe on Allison. Maybe my friend could pick up a psychic hit... anything.

And as we rolled down The Row, with Sherbet trailing behind in his unmarked sedan, and as the sun slid further and further behind the distant horizon, I knew the prospects of finding my son alive slid further and further away, too...

Chapter 32

Anthony ran blindly... and straight into a wooden crate.

The wood cracked and light exploded in his head, and he rebounded, stumbling. When the light dispersed, he saw that one of the arrows had broken in half. He tossed aside the broken arrow, shoved the remaining two in his back pocket, and did the only thing he could think of. He leaped up onto the wooden crate—a crate he seemed to recall was near a bay of massive, industrial-sized shelving.

From the wooden crate, he leaped blindly out into space, praying like crazy that he landed on one of the shelves... and not on one of the yellow-eyed monsters coming at him much faster than anything that big had any right to move...

***

We were more than halfway down The Row, passing slow-moving big rigs, and a steady stream of small trucks and cars, as most workers were heading home for the day.

The sun had set minutes ago—more than enough time for the werewolves to have fully transformed by now... and intent on stalking my son.

Never had I felt so helpless... and so without hope...

***

Anthony's memory hadn't been perfect, but he landed on a wide shelf, and hit his shin on the edge in the process. He yelped and rolled and felt the entire structure shudder beneath his weight.

He held his leg and felt the blood flowing from the gash. He had hit the edge hard. He felt in his back pocket. The two arrows were still there. Anthony might have whimpered. But at least he was one shelf above the first of the creatures to arrive.

Too close, Anthony thought. Just too damn close.

Anthony's searching hands found a metal support beam, and now he was climbing as fast he could. He ignored the pain in his leg that was already healing—and was doing his best to ignore the fact that the structure shuddered again and again.

He was certain that two of the werewolves had leaped onto the shelf just below him.

***

"I hear him, Mommy!"

"Where, Tammy?"

"I-I don't know. But he's close, Mommy. Just keep driving."

"Is he okay?"

"No, Mommy. He's scared. He's running. They're after him!"

***

Anthony found himself high on the upper shelving unit.

He knew this thanks to another flash of light that revealed a long, wide, mostly empty shelf. A few pallets were scattered here and there over the surface. He was, he suspected, many dozens of feet off the ground. Far enough up that the yellow eyes below were only tiny pinpricks of hate and anger. Or hunger.

He was on the edge of the wide shelf. Below was the open area with the feeding chair. Above him, but too far away to reach, would be his creepy math teacher in his swinging, slightly creaking, spruced-up shark cage. No doubt, he was watching him even now. Anthony raised a finger and gave him the bird. From above, Anthony heard a muffled chuckling. Yep, he was watching, all right.

What a creepy prick. Maybe Kingsley will kick the crap out of him, too.

Anthony heard two of them on the shelf below his, scrabbling along the metal unit beneath him, their claws clicking and scratching. They might not be good climbers, according to Matthews, but they might have seen him using the metal support beam —

And they had. The structure shook some more and he heard them climbing, up, up, up. And when the metal shelf beneath his feet sagged, Anthony knew he was no longer alone on this narrow upper platform, a platform that was not more than three or four feet wide. To jump down from this high would result, he knew, in some injury or another. Maybe a broken ankle. Besides, he didn't know where he would land, or on what. So he stayed up there.

A sudden snapshot of light revealed that, yes, there were two of them on the shelf with him, advancing toward him. He saw one actually drool—and click its long, curved claws. Each creature was so hulking and thickly muscled that he knew, without a doubt, they could tear him from limb to limb.

But not without a fight first.

He reached back and removed the two silver-tipped arrows from his back pocket.

***

"There, Mommy!"

"Where?"

"That building there, the one behind the others, the one behind the barb-wired fence."

I saw it—hidden far enough off the street to go unnoticed by just about anyone other than its neighbors.

I yanked the steering wheel hard, cut off a big rig that would have flattened all of us, and shot up a driveway into a mostly-empty parking lot. Allison and Tammy screamed. The three Lichtenstein monsters didn't so much as scream, as grunt irritably.

I continued giving it gas, aiming for the chain-link fence.

"Hang on," I said.

***

Anthony held his ground, an arrow in each hand.

He felt small and insignificant and more scared than he'd ever felt in his entire life. The two little arrows in his hands were laughable, especially when Anthony found himself looking up into the twin pairs of slowly approaching yellow eyes.

The shelving unit shook and shuddered. From above, he heard the shark cage creak as his traitor of a math teacher no doubt found a better position to watch the creepy show below him.

Another flash of light.

Anthony almost wished he hadn't seen the flash of light, that he hadn't just seen the sheer size of the creatures directly before him. If anything, the beasties were too wide to allow for more than one to approach him at a time; they had to line up single file.

And what he saw made his stomach do a flip. A long line of drool hung from the first creature's mouth in front of him, like a dog waiting for a treat. Except that Anthony was the treat. Anthony had never, ever thought of himself as food before, but now, he did, and it sickened him.

The set of amber eyes directly before him lowered, and the boy knew the creature was crouching, getting ready to attack. Anthony crouched, too, in a fighter's pose, and when the yellow eyes sprung forward, Anthony dropped to his back and thrust one of the arrows up. He could not have been more pleased—or horrified—when the arrow sunk deep into the beast's flesh. Anthony kicked his feet up, bucking hard, and sent the creature up and over him. He heard it crash far, far below, howling and screaming and not very happy at all.

Anthony was certain he hadn't killed it. The arrow, if anything, had lodged deep into its guts, which was a nice payback for what they had done to him.

Directly before him, the second creature inched forward.

***

The fence didn't crash down flat like it always did in the movies. Truthfully, this was my first fence-crashing party, and I really hadn't known what to expect, especially driving a damn minivan.

What did happen would just have to be good enough. The fence buckled forward, but the van got hung up on it, back tires spinning. No matter—the building wasn't far away at all.

I gave Tammy strict orders to stay in the van. I commanded one of the Lichtenstein monsters to stay with her and protect her. As luck would have it, the one I commanded had been the one Tammy had been staring at earlier.

I would worry about that later.

With that, I was out my door in a flash, scrambling over the fence, with two of the monsters and Allison following...

***

This second werewolf was more cautious—it seemed aware that Anthony was holding one of the silver-tipped arrows.

As it approached, Anthony felt the shelving shudder again and again. More creatures were climbing up. The problem was... Anthony had just the one arrow. That, and he was only thirteen and these were freakin' monsters. Oh, and he was fighting blind.

Where was the burst of light when he needed it?

He didn't know. He also didn't know what brought on the light, and from where it came. It was just there, willy-nilly, on its own. It seemed random, too. But now, weirdly, the lights were coming more often and staying longer. In the beginning, they had been mere blips.

Still, a fat lot of good that did him now, especially when one of the beasts was closing in on him now...

The light, he thought. *I need the light.*

The second werewolf lashed out a clawed hand —faster and more powerful than Anthony was prepared for. It caught Anthony on his upper right arm and sent him spinning over the wide shelf. He would have spun right off the edge if he hadn't caught one of the metal support beams. As he gasped, blood poured free from what he suspected were three or four really deep gashes. His arm, he was certain, was now useless.

He held it against him, and wanted to cry, but he wouldn't let himself. He couldn't. Not now, and maybe never again.

Anthony watched the yellow eyes moving in their sockets, scanning him. Then the eyes squinted, and the creature let loose with a bladder-emptying roar and leaped forward.

Anthony nearly curled into a ball right then and there. But he didn't curl up. Instead, he did his best to predict where the next swing was coming from and, judging by the fact that the first had been a powerful right roundhouse, he guessed a blow would launch from the creature's shoulder, a straight shot that was probably meant to remove Anthony's head from his shoulders—except that Anthony had already ducked under it. And as he ducked, he lunged forward, and drove the second arrow deep into the creature's chest.

The reaction this time was different. Two massive paws dropped on Anthony's shoulder, limply. The creature threw its head back to roar, except no sound came out. Instead, the thing dropped to his knees, or haunches, whatever they were called. Anthony stepped back as it pitched forward... then rolled off the top shelf, to land heavily with a heavy, bone-crushing thud far below.

I killed it, he thought. *I really killed it.*

Anthony wasn't sure how he felt about killing it, but he was glad that he was still alive.

But now, he was without arrows.

***

I was the first to arrive at the building, which looked completely abandoned. No big rigs, no cars, no activity. If any sound was coming from within, I couldn't hear it, which made me suspect that bastard Matthews had sound-proofed the building.

With the pounding of footsteps behind— heavier pounding from the two Lichtenstein monsters, and the not-so-heavy pounding of Allison

—I cast my thoughts outward. Not just my thoughts, but my inner eye, utilizing a sort of radar/sonar I'd somehow managed to discover years ago. The all-seeing eye expanded in all directions at once, even down twenty or so feet below me, too, if I chose to focus my attention in that direction. I didn't. Instead, I focused in the direction of the building before me.

Little, if anything, could block such sight, as I'd proven to see through cave walls and even the earth itself. In this case, I plunged through the thick cement walls, through additional padding, and soon found myself in an empty room, an office perhaps. Beyond it was a hallway, and beyond that... I couldn't see. I had reached the limits of my "seeing."

But the clear view of the office was enough. I told the others to take hold of my hands and arms, anything they could grab. Allison took a hand, and each of the Lichtenstein monsters grabbed hold of an arm.

Once done, I summoned the single flame.

***

Anthony didn't want to die.

He also didn't want to die in darkness, torn to shreds by monsters that he couldn't even see.

At least give me a fighting chance, he thought. *Give me some light!*

He just needed to see that beautiful burst of

random light. Just one more time. And he needed it to stick around longer, too. Just a few seconds longer—just long enough for him to defend himself.

Anthony wasn't afraid of the werewolves. Not anymore. They were strong and fast, yes, but there was still a chance—the smallest of chances—that he could fend them off until help came.

And he knew, without a shadow of a doubt, that his mother was coming for him. He just needed to give her time.

I need time, he thought, as a new set of yellow eyes appeared on the shelf before him. *Time and light.*

How and why did the flash of light appear? And it wasn't really a flash, was it? No, it was more like a rocketing, squiggly laser beam of light. But it was enough to see, just briefly.

Could he *make* it appear? He didn't know—and it was all so frustrating.

"C'mon, dammit, where are you?" he muttered, recognizing that he was already at the very edge of the shelf. More yellow eyes below him, and yellow eyes in front of him, advanced. Each pair represented a fierce, mindless monster of nightmarish proportions.

"C'mon, c'mon," he whispered. "Where are you?"

In response, he finally did see a light, but not the light he'd expected. No, in the center of his mind, somewhere just behind his forehead—and most definitely in his imagination—he saw a single dancing flame.

Great, he thought. *Just great.*

Yes, his imagination had given him light, but a useless one. He figured it would disappear, but it didn't. It just stayed right there in his thoughts, dancing and flickering. He could see the flame—and he could also see the yellow eyes approaching directly ahead. Soon, they would realize he was weaponless. Perhaps the creatures weren't quite as mindless as he thought. Either way, he wouldn't be able to defend himself in the darkness, not with just one good arm.

And there was that damn single flame, lighting exactly nothing up at all. No, that wasn't true. Something—someone—had stepped *into* the flame. The flame in his mind. Something really, really bright. It was a man. Kind of. A man surrounded in blazing white fire, standing *within* the single yellow flame. And the man was holding two flaming swords. Anthony was sure of it. He was also sure he was losing his mind.

But strangest of all... the man seemed to be looking at Anthony, seemed to be waiting... for something. Now, Anthony felt a beckoning, a calling, a yearning to go to the flame... to go to the man in the flame.

How to go to it, he didn't know.

But going to it—whatever that meant—felt better than standing here and getting torn to pieces by creatures he still couldn't see.

"Go," he heard his father say in his head. "Go

now!"

Anthony felt the pull, felt the connection to the burning man in the flame... he felt himself moving toward the flame, toward the man inside, a man Anthony felt an odd kinship with, for reasons he didn't get, and didn't have time to think about.

The werewolf attacked. And not just one, but two or three of them, bounding over the wide ledge, snarling and scrabbling...

As they came at him, Anthony did two things at the same time: he leaped backward into space—and rushed toward the flame in his mind, toward the fiery man with the fiery swords...

***

An explosion of white light.

One moment he had been falling in darkness, and the next, he was falling in pure white light—the same white light that had been shooting out in beams from the man in the flame. The man in his thoughts.

Anthony had little time to understand what he'd seen or what he felt. He only knew that the ground was coming up fast... and he was going to land square on his back. Maneuvering in a way he'd never thought possible, with control he never knew he had, he flipped his legs up and over his head.

He landed smoothly, effortlessly, on one knee and one foot, his right fist anchoring the ground before him.

His blazing white fist.

***

We were halfway down the hall when we saw the explosion of white light; it poured through the doorway at the far end of the corridor.

I picked up speed, leaving the others behind...

***

Anthony stood, keenly aware that white light was radiating from him, touching everything, especially those hulking creatures who shied away from the light.

Most curiously, Anthony saw that he now towered over these very same monsters. And, yes, they were monsters. Frightening to behold, the things of nightmares.

Except Anthony didn't feel fear. He suspected the fiery man had never known fear. The fiery man who was also him.

He also knew, without a shadow of a doubt, that two fiery swords were sheathed along his back.

He reached for them now, withdrawing them expertly, smoothly, swinging them once, twice, and holding them out before him... two fiery white swords held by fiery white hands.

His hands...

***

Never had Anthony felt so strong, so alive, so invincible. And never had he been so confused, either.

He held up the swords before him. Each crackled with living fire. In fact, there was no boundary between his hands and the swords. Where his fiery hands stopped, the swords began.

Beyond his hands, aglow in white light, he saw two or three of the werewolves shying away, holding up their own hands—or paws, whatever they were. Anthony wasn't sure how werewolves normally looked, but these three seemed confused. They also seemed smaller than he remembered, maybe because he now towered above them.

Towered might not have been accurate. He certainly towered over the boy he had once been. As far as he could tell now, he was a head or two taller than the tallest of the werewolves.

How tall he was now seemed less important than *what* he was. And what he was, he hadn't a clue. Should he be scared? He didn't know. He didn't feel scared. If anything, he felt... eager for battle.

Very, very eager.

He'd worry about what he was later. For now, he was ready for battle. No, he was *hungry* for battle.

Although he had never practiced with swords before except on a friend's Wii—much less these fiery swords—Anthony knew, without a shadow of a doubt, what to do with these weapons, how to strike with them to protect himself, and, most importantly, how to attack with them.

Now, he lowered his hands—and sensed his enemy's anger. The very air around him crackled with the anticipation of an imminent attack. How he knew this, he didn't know, and didn't question it. Not now, and not in this moment.

Anthony grinned, and felt his lips of fire curling up.

Yes, let them attack.

***

I wasn't entirely prepared for what I saw as I rounded the long row of industrial shelving. Hell, no one could have been prepared for it—a massive, burning entity.

It vaguely resembled an angel, or a demon, or something in-between. It wielded two impossibly long swords as deftly as if they had been an extension of its own arms. Maybe they were. After all, the entity and swords were all made of the same pale fire, fire that crackled and sputtered like the surface of the sun, had the sun been white. And like a sun, it emitted its own brilliance, touching everything in all directions.

But the entity wasn't alone. No. In fact, it was surrounded by massive, brutish, muscled, crazy scary-looking creatures that most certainly belonged in nightmares and not in the real world. And nowhere to be seen was my son—I prayed like crazy that it was a good thing.

The others reached me now, with Allison coming up next to me. I caught sight of her pretty face glowing in the white light, her mouth hanging open, sweat on her brow. The Lichtenstein monsters appeared next on my left. They gave no reaction to the burning entity, even as their scarred faces glowed in the burning luminescence. Sherbet came up last, holding his chest and praying under his breath. I didn't blame him.

A hulking, nightmarish creature dashed forward, leaping high into the air, its claws bared, lips pulled back to reveal two rows of hellish teeth. The burning man slashed upward, flicking his wrist so fast that I almost believed I imagined it. What I didn't imagine was the werewolf's head that veritably leaped from the creature's shoulders and rolled across the open floor, coming to a stop against what appeared to be a single chair with handcuffs attached to the arms.

More of the werewolves sprang forward—and Allison grabbed my hand, pulling me. But I didn't move, couldn't move. I stood, transfixed. More creatures dropped from above, although none seemed aware of our presence just yet. All were dealt with swiftly and efficiently. More heads leaped free. Some bodies were rendered in half, and almost all lost limbs in the process.

One creature fled the fire entity—and charged toward us. Allison raised her hands, braced herself.

I braced myself, too. I knew the kind of witchy power she could yield. But the two Lichtenstein monsters were already moving, springing forward. One tackled the beast down low, while the other tackled high. The three rolled and rolled, and when they stopped rolling, there was a dagger hilt projecting from the creature's chest.

It was all terrible and fascinating—but never once did I stop looking for my son, who was nowhere to be found. Nowhere at all.

Before us, the fiery creature dispatched the last of the werewolves with a final, diagonal slash of its blade, a cut that severed the creature in half from one hip and up to the shoulder. I tried to ignore the splash of guts hitting the floor.

The burning entity held both hands out, both swords crossed before it, and seemed to be satisfied that it had vanquished the monsters. Now, it turned slowly—ever so slowly—in our direction.

"Samantha, what do we do?" asked Allison.

I swallowed. I hadn't the faintest idea.

Chapter 33

Allison took my hand.

The two Lichtenstein monsters had stepped aside, their faces aglow in white light. Their hair, I noted, lifted and rose from an unseen wind. The burning entity spun his swords deftly, easily, and re-sheathed them along his back. What, exactly, he re-sheathed them into, I didn't know. From here, I could see the burning handles of each blade rising over its shoulders, ready for quick access.

"Sam..." said Allison.

"Be cool," I said.

"What is it?"

"I don't know."

"Sam, I'm going to pee my pants."

"That's not being cool."

The thing approached us slowly, cautiously, curiously, carefully. And the closer it got, the more

Allison danced next to me. I thought she really was going to pee herself. There was something about the way it moved, about the way it seemed to be looking at me...

"Wait here," I said, and released her hand. "And don't pee yourself."

***

It could have been a mini-sun.

So much heat, and wind, too. Hot dry wind that smelled of burning sulfur. And the sound coming off it... I was reminded of sizzling bacon, or sizzling skin.

I approached slowly, working through more emotions than I thought was possible to feel at one time. I had once heard that a person couldn't feel love and fear at the same time. But I wasn't so sure that was true. At least, not now and not in this situation.

The faceless entity seemed to be watching me, following my progress toward it, angling his head slightly as I approached.

Although it appeared to be made entirely of fire, it had to have a core, some physicality. Indeed, something with weight and heft had wielded the sword... surely there was a physical body there somewhere beneath the flames, although it really didn't matter in this moment. Not when the thing before me slouched in a familiar way, shoulders hunched, arms hanging down awkwardly at his waist.

I shook my head and didn't fight the tears. The smell of blood and singed hair was in the air, and something else, too. Something foreign to me. The smell of molten rock, perhaps. Or molten metal. A white tongue of flame erupted along the fire entity's bicep, snapping and crackling, and then disappeared again. Like a solar flare. The entity didn't seem to notice, which was really no surprise as smaller such flares were continuously erupting over its burning surface.

Sweat from the heat broke out on my brow, and, with the sizzling sound of frying bacon drowning out every other sound in the warehouse, I said, "Hi, baby."

***

The entity nodded. No, my *son* nodded.

"You can hear me?" I asked. "Understand me?"

Another nod. Long and slow and purposeful.

"Did they... did they hurt you, baby?" I asked.

The entity—Anthony—seemed undecided, then finally shook his massive, burning head. He wasn't hurt, but something had happened. They had tried to hurt him, maybe. But they couldn't, not really. Still, I wanted to kill them all over again. But slowly.

"Are you scared, baby?" I asked.

After a long moment, the burning head nodded. As it did so, a liquefied drop of molten fire dripped from its chin and evaporated halfway to the ground.

"You're afraid," I said, and he nodded again, and more burning drops of fire sprang free, raining down around me. Burning up before they actually hit me.

I wanted to hug him, but the fire was real—the intense heat of it was enough for me to believe that. I reached out a hand, then dropped it again; instead, I took a step forward.

"It's going to be okay, baby..."

He hung his head, and more molten drops dripped from his chin. And now, he covered his face with his hand—and face and hands were briefly indistinguishable.

I understood his pain. It didn't matter that they were going to kill him or, or that they were monsters of the worst kind, I knew my boy, and the emotions of the day, the evening, of fighting for his life, of killing, were overwhelming to him. Would have been overwhelming to anyone.

I let him weep his liquid fire, and still, I inched closer to him, as close as I dared. My hair blew back. Some of it even melted, I suspected. Maybe the loose strands. I felt my own T-shirt sticking to my skin, felt the buttons of my jeans heating to a nuclear temperature. At least, that's how it felt against my skin.

My son, I thought. *What have I done to you?*

I suspected what had happened—and now, it was time to undo what had happened.

***

"Anthony, baby, I need you to look at me."

He did, dropping his hand from his face and standing straighter. He seemed to inhale, although I doubted he needed any air. Not in this form.

"You saw the single flame," I said.

He tilted his head one way, then the other.

I elaborated: "You saw the single flame in your thoughts. And you also saw the fire man inside the flame."

Now, Anthony was nodding, slowly.

"Good, sweetie. Now, I need you to think about the flame again—that is, try to imagine it again. Try to do it now, okay, sweetie?"

He tilted his head again, but then, finally nodded.

I waited a moment or two before saying, "Do you see the flame now?"

Another nod.

"Good, baby. You're doing real good, and it's going to be okay, I promise. Now, see yourself in the flame. See yourself as the thirteen-year-old boy you were today. Do your best."

I waited again, and now, Anthony was nodding, this time excitedly. He saw himself in the flame. I could almost cry. In fact, I was.

"You are doing so good, sweetie. Now... feel yourself move toward the flame. You can do it, baby. You can do it."

He stopped nodding, and had just tilted his head when he seemed to wink out of existence. I found myself blinded by the sudden disappearance of the white light. Black spots swam before me, and as I held out my hands, searching, and found another set of hands. Hands I knew well.

I pulled Anthony into me and held him tighter than I'd ever held him before.

Chapter 34

Minutes later, I saw the interior of the cage within my own internal flame, and, in a disorienting blink, I found myself high above the warehouse floor, swinging and creaking with Mr. Matthews.

There was a chair welded into place, along with a control panel that sported a couple of buttons and switches. In the far corner, huddled and watching me with wide, crazy eyes, was the man I now knew as Mr. Matthews.

I delved into his mind, saw what he knew, saw that he'd been able to see auras his whole life, saw his partnership with the local wolf pack, saw all of his terrible efforts in acquiring this abandoned warehouse, acquiring this crane, the lengths he went to in building the staging room, this protective cage, and wiring the control panel. Mostly, I felt his craziness and bloodlust. His hunger was to see suffering, to understand it. He had convinced himself that it was for scientific purposes, but he was just a crazy whack job who had only tried to justify his actions that showed his complete lack of empathy for the human condition. He was a full-blown sociopath.

The entity within me could understand the man before me. Hell, I sensed her kinship with him. A man who cared little for other humans, who used them for his own sick entertainment. But the mother in me trumped the bitch inside me every time.

"Ms. Moon," he said.

"Mr. Matthews," I said.

"You were reading my mind," he said.

"I was."

"You know everything, I presume."

"You presume correctly."

"You can't take any of this to the police."

"I know," I said.

He nodded. We creaked high in the air. Below, the two Lichtenstein monsters were cleaning up the mess. Turned out that Mr. Matthews had also built a handy, large crematorium on the premises, as well. Allison and Anthony were outside, with Tammy and Sherbet and the third Lichtenstein monster.

"You are a vampire."

"So they say."

"And your son?"

"He's something else," I said. "Something in-between. Something very special. Something alive and well, no thanks to you."

He looked a little embarrassed. "When you say it like that, I sound like a monster. I'm just trying to understand what these creatures are, their habits, their needs, their preferences."

"And in return, you get a good show."

"I suspect you know what I get in return."

"It's time for you to go now," I said.

"Go where?"

I snatched his hand and he squeaked like a tiny mouse as I summoned the single flame again. This time, I saw within it a place I had never ventured before, a place I'd never thought I would be. A place I had seen once, through a barred window.

***

Kingsley's cell smelled like wide-open ass.

It also smelled like something rotting and putrid and about as dead as dead could be. When I regained my balance, I blinked and saw the rotted corpse of what appeared to be a small deer, a corpse that was overflowing with guts and maggots.

A shaggy, filthy head looked up from its chest cavity, dripping blood and little white worms from his muzzle—a hulking creature that was easily head and shoulders taller than the same such creatures I had seen tonight. Kingsley was, by far, the biggest of them all. The growl that erupted from him was terrifying, and I might have peed a little, too.

I knew from experience—and present evidence —that my boyfriend preferred the rotting over the living. I doubted he would consume the math teacher. Render him into a human jigsaw puzzle, yes. Eat him, no. At least, I hoped he wouldn't.

I released Matthews' hands, summoned the single flame again, and saw within it the exterior of the warehouse. I teleported away just as the hulking, filthy creature who was my boyfriend leaped over the bloated deer and lunged at us. As frightening a sight as I'd ever seen.

Apparently, Matthews agreed. He screamed and tried to grab my hand, but I was already gone.

Good riddance.

Chapter 35

"What do we tell the press? The community? The school? Parents are going to want answers, Sam. People are scared. This kidnapping has made national headlines. Hell, world headlines."

I stood with Sherbet outside his unmarked vehicle. No flashing lights, no other law enforcement. Inside the warehouse, the Lichtenstein monsters were still disposing of the slaughtered beasts.

Sherbet had been caught up to speed. That's the good thing with this telepathy business. I needed only to give him access to the memories I wanted him to see; in this case, the memory of Matthews in Kingsley's cell. Sherbet didn't like it, but he also knew that he was knee-deep in the supernatural.

I said, "We tell the press that Anthony escaped his kidnappers. He was found walking along the side of the road."

"And the kidnappers?"

"They escaped."

"There will be a nationwide hunt."

"Let them look."

"Others will want to talk to Anthony... federal agencies, doctors, therapists. He will need to keep his story straight—"

"My son is no stranger to keeping secrets. I will talk to him."

Sherbet took in a lot of air... and blew it out loudly through his mouth. "Jesus, Sam."

"I know."

I looked past him, to my son sitting in the back seat of Sherbet's unmarked white sedan. With head bowed, my son, if anything, looked miserable.

Lots of therapy, I thought. *Lots and lots of therapy.*

Except... who could he talk to?

"And what about Angie Sanderson's parents?" asked Sherbet. "We found her killers. We now know what happened to her. Now, her parents could have closure... except..."

Except it wasn't the kind of closure they could know about—or anyone could know about. I nodded. I had been thinking about them, too. They deserved closure. I said, "I'll talk to her parents, too."

"And tell them what?"

"I'll let them know that their daughter's killers were found and dealt with. I'll tell them she died peacefully."

"But she didn't."

I shook my head. "Her parents don't need to know that."

"Let me guess," said Sherbet. "And they won't remember talking to you, either."

"No, they won't."

"How will this work, Sam?"

I shrugged. "I'll tell them that they need never discuss her abduction again. Others will honor it."

"Will you take away their pain?"

"As much as possible."

***

"Hi, baby," I said, slipping into the seat next to him and closing the car door behind me.

"I'm not a baby, Mom."

"Do you want me to stop calling you baby?"

He thought about it, scrunching up his face the way he sometimes did, and then shrugged. "Maybe someday."

"But not today?"

He glanced at me. "No, not today."

"Let me see your stomach again."

He sat back, lifted up his shirt. The wound had scabbed over, but it was still significant. Already it was better than when I'd first seen it about an hour or so ago.

"Sweetie, how long have you known about..."

"The fire warrior?"

"Yes, him."

He shrugged. "I didn't. Not until I saw the flame."

"How did you know what to do next?"

"Daddy told me," Anthony said, smiling. "Well, the voice of Daddy told me."

I blinked and suddenly felt very, very cold. "Daddy?"

"Yes."

"Do you often hear Daddy's voice?"

Another shrug. "Not at first. I mean, not right after he was killed. But more and more lately."

"Do you think it's really Daddy?"

Anthony looked at me, and his pupils dilated a little, and behind them, I thought I detected a glimmer of fire. Then, he smiled broadly and said, "Of course not, Mommy. It's just my imagination."

Chapter 36

"You rang, Samantha Moon?"

I hadn't. I had shouted out into the night for the bastard to meet me here, at the Amtrak station in downtown Fullerton, where it was bustling and lively, with lots of places to sit and chat. Although I intended to do a lot more than chat with him.

The man I now knew as the devil sauntered through the crowded courtyard, past waiting passengers, young professionals, and students—all of whom were staring down at their smartphones— oblivious to the devil in their presence. I was sitting near a gurgling fountain, which should give us enough cover to talk.

"Good work finding your son, Ms. Moon. You are indeed an ace detective."

"Apparently, you found him first."

"Not so much found him as was led to him."

"By your hellhound."

"He's a good doggie."

"How long have you known about Anthony and his dad?"

"Not very long, Samantha Moon. Shortly before your own arrival at the warehouse, in fact."

"How did you find him? Danny, that is?"

The devil studied me, then shrugged. "Your ex-hubby has been revealing himself more and more to your son. Speaking to him, whispering to him, helping him. By rising up through the depths to speak to your son, your ex-husband was no longer in hiding."

"And your dog can hear him?" I asked.

"Dogs. And in a way, yes."

"Fine," I said. "My son said you helped him. Why?"

"Ah, a sticky point, Samantha Moon. I don't like sticky points, truth be known. I lean toward neat and clean and easy. But, yes, your son is a rare breed."

I didn't like where this was going.

"Then I will just remove Danny," I said, "and you can just go back to hell."

"Will you now, Sam?"

I opened my mouth, but then stopped short. I would remove Danny... if I could. Except I'd never had access to my own son's mind. Nor did I have access to other immortals' minds, if that was what my son was. A double whammy.

"Your conundrum is only now occurring to

you, I see. Sadly, you can't remove Danny Moon from your own son. You see, I know a thing or two about vampires, what vile creatures they are. Present company excluded, of course. I know, for instance, they don't have access to other immortals' minds."

A train came to a screeching, howling stop, horn blowing, brakes squealing. People boarded, and even more unloaded. Many swept past us toward the parking lot beyond. Many looked like they had places to go. Others not so much. Others looked like lost souls. I was reminded of Dracula's blood servant, whom I had fetched earlier in the evening. The woman—her name was Constance—was presently sound asleep in Allison's guest bedroom in Beverly Hills. We would figure out what to do with her tomorrow. For now, she was safe.

"Your ex-hubby has plans for your son, Sam. Big plans. And I assure you, they are not good. No, not at all. In fact, I quite admire the direction he is taking things. But there's another wrinkle. Ah, I see you know where I'm going with this."

I did know. I sensed it the moment that Anthony had first mentioned hearing his dad's voice.

"Your son quite likes having Daddy around."

I said nothing. I sat there and breathed and fought an urge to leap across the table and smack the smug look off the devil's face before me. No, tear it off. Mostly, I sat there and realized that there was nothing I could do. At least, not now.

"I see I have given you a lot to think about, Samantha Moon. Once again, I am glad your son is safe. And you're welcome."

I blinked. "Welcome for what?"

"Those handcuffs didn't uncuff themselves, Sam. It was, after all, the least I could do. Now, I have a train to catch."

I blinked and opened my mouth to speak, but closed it again. The devil stood, tipped an invisible hat and sauntered off toward the tracks. There was a train coming, but it wasn't slowing; apparently, this wasn't its scheduled stop.

The devil vaulted over a metal railing and fell down onto the tracks, directly in the path of the oncoming train.

The horn blew and brakes squealed, but far too late.

The body of the man named Buck Taggart exploded into a million bloody pieces. And, as people screamed and an alarm sounded, I watched as an oily, dragon-like shadow rose up from the tracks, circled once, and disappeared up into the night.

The End

About the Author:

J.R. Rain is an ex-private investigator who now writes full-time. He lives in a small house on a small island with his small dog, Sadie. Please visit him at www.jrrain.com.

CPSIA information can be obtained
at www.ICGtesting.com
Printed in the USA
BVHW040925171118
533363BV00019B/507/P

9 781535 284400